HOW TO WOO A WARRIOR ORC

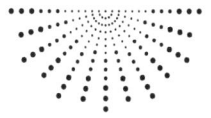

JANUARY BELL

HOW TO WOO A WARRIOR ORC

Cover by Book Brander Boutique, illustration by Kateryna www.romancepremades.com

Published by January Bell

www.januarybellromance.com

Copyright © 2024 January Bell

This is a work of fiction. Unless otherwise indicated, all the names, characters, businesses, places, events and incidents in this book are either the product of the author's imagination or used in a fictitious manner. Any resemblance to actual persons, living or dead, or actual events is purely coincidental.

All rights reserved. No portion of this book may be reproduced in any form without permission from the publisher, except as permitted by U.S. copyright law. For permissions contact: admin@januarybellromance.com

For sub-rights inquiries, please contact Jessica Watterson at Sandra Djikstra Literary Agency.

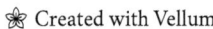 Created with Vellum

AUTHOR'S NOTE

The stakes will be low, the spice will be hot, and the men will be monstrous— but only in the best ways.

For a full list of content warnings and an introduction please visit the Wild Oak Woods website.

CHAPTER ONE

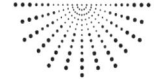

PIPER

The roses are about to be in bloom.

I stare at them, a muscle in my eye twitching, knowing I should be pleased. The roses that climb over the sign proclaiming The Pixie's Perch, and are currently positively littered with buds, are beautiful.

They smell amazing.

My eye twitches again, and I rub my palm across my face, only succeeding in smearing flour all over my nose.

"What's wrong?" a deep, familiar voice murmurs from behind me, and I nearly jump out of my skin.

I should be used to Ga'Rek, the orc I hired to assist with my increasingly absurd baking load.

I should be pleased about the last flush of roses.

I should be both of those things, and I am very much not.

"They look like summer," I finally admit, burying my face in my hands. "The fall festival is in one week, and it's going to look like summer."

Velvet nuzzles her soft nose against my hip, my deer familiar clearly unhappy that I'm unhappy—which just makes me feel worse.

"It's going to look like magic. Like everything else you do," Ga'Rek tells me. His big hand grazes against the small of my back, and a delicious shiver goes through me at the thought that he's just touching me to comfort me.

Until I realize he's tugging at my apron strings, which drag on the cobblestones behind me, barely visible in the early morning gloam. It's darker than it has been at this time for months, and usually that would thrill me.

Autumn is by far my favorite of all the seasons. My mother used to say that the fairies painted the leaves in crimson and burnt umber while we slept. The flush of fall color on foliage reminds me of her, and those happy mornings we spent baking while she told me stories of the fair folk and taught me long-held secrets of kitchen witchery.

His fingers brush against my back again as he ties my apron on for me, surprisingly adept considering how large they are.

"Thank you," I murmur, slightly off balance from his proximity.

I half-turn, the rag I've planned to use to clean the windows swinging uselessly in my hands.

"Couldn't have the finest pastry chef in all the region tripping and falling on her apron ribbons," he tells me in a low rumble.

Ga'Rek's smile transforms his typical orc-ish resting glower to an expression of pure joy, and, as it always does, elicits a smile of my own in response.

His hand brushes across my hip as he finishes tying the strings.

I shiver in response, goosebumps rising across my bare arms.

No, not in response—more likely from the chill pre-dawn breeze that signals the true demise of summer and beginning of fall. Soon, green will be replaced on the leaves all around us as they melt into fiery oranges and reds before the boughs lose them with a great shake and go to sleep for winter.

Not that the budding roses dripping dramatically over the front of my pastry shop received the autumnal notice.

Tears of frustration sting my eyes, and I sniff once, outraged by my own irrational outrage. Two outrages for the price of one.

"Do not cry, kal'aki ne," Ga'Rek murmurs, so low I nearly miss the words. "We will make it right."

I rub the back of my hand across one eye. I don't know what the name he keeps calling me means, and I'm half afraid to ask.

Probably something like, 'weak worm' or 'possible appetizer' or 'tiny snack' or 'woman who cries over roses for no damned good reason.'

Could be any of those things.

I open my mouth to ask.

"Do you miss speaking Orcish?" comes out instead.

Ga'Rek goes silent, and I'm a coward, because I can't even bring myself to look at him.

Finally, I wipe the one spot I've missed on the window, the glass squeaking under my ministrations. The willow broom I keep beside the door out of pure witch tradition seems to glare at me in reproach for my rude question.

Even Velvet seems to side-eye me from where she stands, grazing on some of the potted impatiens that flank my shop. It's time to switch them out to something more appropriate for fall. The roses are clearly beyond my control, but the annuals? The annuals I can at least make festive.

"Orcish isn't just something spoken," Ga'Rek finally answers.

A blush heats my cheeks. "I, I didn't mean to pry, please don't feel like you have to answer—"

"Language doesn't cease to exist just because it isn't spoken. It lives inside our hearts and minds. And how could I miss it when I just spoke it to you?" A laugh follows the question, and though there's not a shred of cruelty or fun-making in it, my cheeks get even hotter.

Stammering an apology, I open the front door and practically jog inside. Black and white checkered tiles run together as I race towards the kitchen in the back, needing to splash water on my cheeks and get myself right before Ga'Rek and I start our work together.

I should be used to the huge orc by now, should be used to the way he seems to know exactly where to move around me in the kitchen. It's a specific dance of companions, when you know how to predict where they will be at any given moment, how to determine where their tasks will take them.

It should have taken us much, much longer to reach this point of comfort with each other than the few meager weeks that have passed.

The thought makes me feel wildly uncomfortable, and then it gets so much worse, because it's immediately followed by a very obvious realization.

This huge warrior orc who's made himself at home here in my most sacred space, my kitchen… I am extremely attracted to him.

And there's nothing friendly or companionable about it.

I swallow hard, squeezing my eyes shut as the bell over the door jingles, announcing he's followed me inside The Pixie's Perch.

The question is now: what am I going to do about it?

CHAPTER TWO

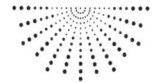

GA'REK

I slipped.

Using Orcish has clearly frightened Piper, who all but sprinted away from me. She's as flighty as the pixies she's named her shop after, and as shy and sweet as her deer familiar.

I take my time strolling to the back of her café, enjoying, as always, the scent of the place. Cinnamon and lavender, sugar and butter, the unmistakable earthy smell of yeast dough rising.

The sun-drenched Pixie's Perch, with its quaint mismatched furniture, is a far cry from the darkly glamorous world of the Underhill. No, the brass and glass candle pendants that hang from the ceiling and glow softly aren't the cold-lit diamond chandeliers the Dark Queen of the Unseelie prefers, and I am glad for it.

I close my eyes, stopping before I enter the kitchen, and soak up the warmth of the morning sun streaming in earnest through the glass windows and onto my back. I would have gotten here earlier, as I normally do, but Piper chewed her lip yesterday afternoon and told me she needed "alone time" with the yeast doughs this morning.

I assumed she meant alone time for herself, period, but from the way she's now chanting over the bowls of colorful cloth-covered dough, perhaps she did mean alone time with the rising dough.

Kitchen witchery, it turns out, is a strange and convoluted magic.

The pink doorframe that leads to the back kitchen creaks as I lean against it.

She doesn't look up from her work, now humming something under her breath as she pulls a ball of sticky dough out.

"I could go down to Willow's Apothecary and see if she has anything in her greenhouse to add to the front porch for, uh, autumn, if you'd like." I'm fishing for words, for a solution to her distress.

Despite me comforting her only a few days ago in her friend Wren's small living room, promising her she did not have to handle the fall festival and the duchess's visit to Wild Oak Woods, Piper has shunned all attempts to lighten her load.

It's frustrating and endearing all at once.

The petite woman is clearly not used to asking for or receiving help of any kind, and I can't help but marvel at the weight she bears on those slim shoulders.

Piper doesn't answer, simply keeps humming to her dough.

"I could see if Willow has something to make the roses look… more harvest festival worthy?" To tell the truth, I don't understand why the roses have sent Piper into a stress spiral. The deep green leaves and what look to be deep pink blossoms look lovely against the striped awning over the glass window.

It doesn't matter what I think, though, not in this case.

If Piper thinks the roses will ruin her harvest festival, then I will fix the roses.

"Willow won't touch the roses," she finally answers, startling me from my quiet reverie. She's blinking up at me, as if surprised to find me here. Her lush lips are slightly parted, her deeper pink tongue flicking out to catch what appears to be a stray bit of sugar.

"Her plant magic," she pauses, her nostrils flaring as she inhales, "isn't to be used for aesthetic purposes."

I blink at her bitter tone. "I take it you have asked her... to use it for aesthetic purposes?" I finally venture.

"It has come up," she replies with another sniff.

I bite my cheeks as laughter threatens. "Right. Well. If magicking the roses is off the table, maybe you'd like for me to just rip them out by the roots? We could use them in a bonfire."

My fingers flex at the prospect of doing something violent for once.

Not that I miss being at the murderous beck and call of the Underhill Queen, but sometimes... I do miss, ah, the ole fight or two.

I frown, cracking my knuckles.

A strange choked sputter echoes across the hard kitchen surfaces, and I glance at the tea kettle at the stove before realizing the noise is coming from Piper.

"You are not pulling out my roses," she says vehemently.

I stare at her, confused by what it is she wants, confused by how much I want to solve her problems for her, and confused by what, exactly, it is she's upset about.

"I won't pull them out," I tell her when it becomes clear she's waiting for me to answer.

She harrumphs, her freckled nose wrinkled adorably, a lock of her deep brown hair escaping the velvet ribbon she's tied it back with.

My fingers itch to tuck it back where it belongs.

Strange.

I glance down at them, mildly concerned.

A long breath sends the lock of hair wafting into the air, and she plops the bread down on the marble board she's been kneading it on, giving me her full attention.

Her blue eyes are full of tears.

"Kal'aki ne, why do you cry?" I ask gently, stepping into the warm kitchen. "What can I do?"

I feel more helpless than ever before in my life.

"Oh, Ga'Rek," she sobs, and before I know what's happening, she's rushed to me.

Flour clouds the air as her aproned body slams into mine, her tiny arms doing their best to wrap around my waist.

I hold stock still, unsure how to respond to this. Her little chest shakes, her head barely coming up to the top of my ribs, tears wetting the fabric of my shirt.

Dots swim in front of my eyes, puzzling me, before I realize I'm holding my breath.

Holding my breath, because I'm afraid that breathing too hard will scare this lovely person away, like she's the pixie in question. A wild bird of a woman.

A shaky breath draws my concern, though, driving me to put my huge hands gently on her back. For a long moment, she just holds me, until her crying quiets.

Carefully, I pat her back.

Once, when I was a very small orc-child, I found a bird with a broken wing. I made a nest for it in a hollowed out log, far enough from my home that my parents would not find it, were they to bother looking for me.

I took care of it for two weeks, feeding it worms and bugs and berries until it was able to get around for itself.

She feels like that bird in my palms.

The fluttering heart beneath the fragile structure of her ribs, the small breaths.

A little sigh escapes her, fluttering against my stomach like the wings of that same bird.

I am afraid to hold her too tight.

I am afraid of what that means.

"Thank you," she finally says, smiling up at me with watery eyes. She brushes her knuckles against her cheekbone, dashing the remainder of the moisture from her peachy skin. "I really needed a hug."

With that, her arms fall from my hips, and she turns back towards the dough, the occasional sniffle punctuating her low, steady hum as the familiar brush of her magic tingles against my skin.

She's back to working like nothing happened.

Like hugging someone, especially an orc, is as ordinary as breathing.

Meanwhile, I can hardly function. My heart's hammering in my chest, my skin's on fire, and I'm sure if I found a mirror, my normally sage-toned cheeks would be pine-green.

Breathe.

I never once in my life thought I would have to remind myself to breathe.

But here I am, in a witch's deliciously scented kitchen, turned to complete breathless putty by the mere brush of her cheek against my body.

It's a good thing I call myself a warrior no longer, because I don't think I could withstand any attack from this woman, much less another embrace.

CHAPTER THREE

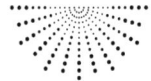

PIPER

*U*sually, it's easy to lose myself in the daily minutiae of running The Pixie's Perch.

Making the baked goods as the sun rises, double checking the cleanliness of the small eat-in area, refreshing the enchantments on the very expensive glass counters to keep everything fresh, and writing the day's menu on the huge board enchanted to update pricing automatically based on the cost of supplies and business overhead.

A neat bit of work, that.

Normally, I'd grin every time the nifty board shifted the prices, but today, all I feel is dread.

I smile at my regulars, put on a pleasant face, and manage to make it through the morning rush without any major stumbles.

My business has always been my anchor, the one thing I've felt I'm good at, baking and kitchen witchery and customer service as natural as breathing.

A cold sweat breaks out between my shoulders, and I clench my jaw.

"Brie and ham sandwiches on pretzel dough coming through," Ga'Rek says quietly from behind me, and I paste a smile on my face as I step out of his way.

I lean against the prep counter. The butcher paper and colorful twine and embossing seals for packaging up orders lay in neat compartments, ready to be used, and I try to do the same to my wayward emotions.

"Piper," Ga'Rek intones, raising an eyebrow at me. "You are not yourself," he says.

And just like that, I want to hug him again.

He smells the way autumn itself should: like pumpkin squares and cinnamon, like ginger cookies with sugared tops, like apple cider and dark, hot chocolate all rolled into one.

I want to run into his wall of muscle and soak up the way he feels and smells until I'm stuffed with it, until it replaces the bleak, stressed out darkness inside me with all the ways I should be feeling right now.

I want to so very badly. My feet take a step towards him, and I grip the counter behind me with both hands to keep from touching him.

I shouldn't.

It's not fair for me to seek comfort from him, an orc who works for me.

Highly inappropriate.

I bite my lip, staring up at him, feeling sad and desperate and not at all like myself.

"Is this still about the festival?" he asks, his green forehead furrowed.

The concern clear on his face makes me melt, and some of that darkness inside me dissipates. I nod, not trusting the tight knot in my throat enough to speak.

"What do you need me to do?" he asks, and I recognize some of that desperation I feel in his words.

I shake my head, unwilling to put it on him. "I don't pay you enough to demand any more work from you."

His expression darkens, and his lips pull back, exposing the tusks I almost forget are there, because they're just part of him.

Now, though, with them on full display, I tilt my head, fascinated by them.

I take a step closer, just to get a better look–

And squeak as his arms wrap back around me, pulling me tight.

"Do you need a hug?" he asks, his voice a low, delicious rumble against where my cheek's pressed against him.

I breathe him in, inhaling that wonderful smell, and the tension that's left bean-sized knots across my back starts to dissolve.

I bury my face in his shirt, my hands automatically going to the small of his back, which is about as high as I come up on him.

By the moon, he makes me feel *safe*.

I snuggle closer, and a low moan comes out of him. I stiffen, worried I've hurt him somehow, maybe exacerbated an old battle injury. I've seen the scars that lace down his sides when his shirt exposes his muscled torso.

It would be hard *not* to notice his torso.

It would be even harder not to notice the fact that, ah, something between his legs is growing larger.

Larger, and much, much harder, until it's pressing against my thigh.

Distracted and flustered, every single anxious thought practically flies away.

It would be so easy to just rub myself against him like a cat, look up at him and bat my lashes, and see if he can make me forget for a bit longer.

When the bell over the door jangles, I practically leap off of him, dismayed by how quickly my resolve to keep things polite and professional has evaporated with two lovely hugs.

"I, uh, I, um. Sorry," I stammer, then whip around to the front door. "Welcome to The Pixie's Perch," I practically scream at the poor, unsuspecting customer.

My eyes close.

Very smooth. Nonchalant, even.

Ga'Rek makes a rumbling noise that might be a laugh, but I'm too embarrassed to even look at him.

Instead, I force myself to stare, wide-eyed and manic, at the woman who's wandered into the shop.

She blinks, then glances around.

"Hope you're hungry!" I make myself chirp at her. "We have the best charmed and enchantment-free baked goods in town."

The Pixie's Perch is the only enchanted edibles café in town too, but that's beside the point.

Ga'Rek moves away from me, heading back towards the kitchen.

I very pointedly keep my manic smile in place as I stare at the newcomer.

"Uh, yes, I am hungry, actually," she says slowly. Coppery brown hair falls around her face, which is gaunt, cheekbones standing out in stark contrast. Dark circles purple the delicate skin under her eyes.

"Sit, sit," I tell her, worry for this too-thin stranger replacing all the embarrassing feelings of unacted upon desire. "I'll bring you a sandwich and a pastry and some hot tea, alright?"

"I don't know if I can—" She glances up at the board behind me, and suddenly, my satisfaction with the magicked prices dries up. "I'm not sure I have enough—"

"On the house," I tell her firmly. "Sit. We all need kindness now and then. I have a knack for knowing when people need it."

The latter isn't true, not in a witchy sense, really. But this woman looks bone-tired, and she's clearly worried about paying me, and I'm not about to let her leave my café hungry. Next to me, Velvet nuzzles my hip and then wanders off to the where the woman sits, fidgeting, at my favorite pink polka-dotted corner table.

"A deer?" she asks in wonder.

"She's my familiar," I tell her. "Velvet. And I'm Piper. Do you like brie and ham?" I pause, pouring hot water into one of the sturdy mugs I prefer to use in the café.

Upstairs, in my little home, I like the thinnest, most feminine and absolutely unnecessary teacups possible. Unfortunately, my lovely teacups aren't minotaur or centaur or troll friendly. Not that we get many trolls.

"That sounds so good," the woman says on a sigh.

I glance over at her, concern making me narrow my eyes.

Velvet's put her long brown face in her lap, her ears pricked up as the woman gingerly strokes my familiar's face.

Happiness washes over me, and I hum to myself as I place a chamomile tea strainer in the mug, smudges of color staining the steaming water.

This is why I do this.

This is why I wake up when it's dark and sunless and cold.

Because food, making a meal for others, making a pastry that helps soothe a soul… it makes me happy.

It fills that aching emptiness that yawns deep inside me, and shores it up with light and companionship.

It's been enough, at least, I thought it has…

I wrap the sandwich in brown wax paper, slicing it in half for neater eating, and in case she wants to take half with her. A jar of pickles sits on the counter, and I fish one out with the silvered tongs my mother loved so dearly.

Funny how a thing like using pickle tongs can summon a memory so strong I nearly feel my mother's gentle touch on the back of my neck.

I shiver, pausing, and when I turn back to the woman in the corner, she's staring at me with wide eyes.

A sense of uncanniness tingles down my spine, all my hair standing up on my arms.

It's not abnormal, per se, to feel touched by a spirit, especially as the veil thins the closer Samhain comes. But this is more than that.

It feels like my mother is here.

My throat tightens and I glance around, knowing she can't be, but looking all the same.

"Do you see her?" the woman asks in a hushed tone. "Tell me you can see her."

Ahhhh. I nod to myself, the woman's appearance suddenly making perfect sense. She's frightened, and Violet nudges her with her nose, the woman automatically petting the deer again.

"What do you see?" I ask her in an even, calm tone.

Outside, thunder rumbles, close enough to shake the glass, and the woman in the corner jumps at the noise.

"Nothing," she says quickly, dropping her gaze to the pink polka dots on the table. "I should go."

"Nonsense," I tell her sternly. "It's about to pour."

No sooner have I said the words than the comforting pitter patter of rain begins to ping on the glass.

I sigh, the woman staring up at me with huge, terrified eyes.

No wonder the store is still near-empty—anyone with any sense has stayed home as the storm brewed above Wild Oak Woods.

"The storm has nothing to do with what you're seeing, and neither do I," I tell her gently, bringing her a heavy plate laden with a sandwich and pickle, as well as some deep-fried potato slices that Ga'Rek loves to make, and my customers love to eat.

"How... how do you know what I'm seeing?" Her face turns so pale that the remnants of summer freckles stand out. "I'm not seeing anything."

She says the last part so fast and looks down at Velvet in a way that tells me very clearly that she is lying, and that she is not a good liar.

I set the plate down in front of her.

"Ga'Rek," I call out. "No need to make more sandwiches. Come have lunch with us."

"I was working on something else," he yells from the kitchen. "I made it for you."

My heart squeezes, and I stare at the arched opening to the kitchen. "You made me something? What?"

"You'll see," he grumbles. "Might be an abomination."

He emerges holding a plate piled high with the deep-fried potatoes—except they're smothered in melted cheese, and…

"Is that… bacon pieces? And green onions?" I ask, confused. It smells amazing. It's a far cry from the usual hunk of bread and jam I scarf down, and my stomach grumbles.

I think I forgot to eat today.

"You need food," he tells me, setting it down on the pink polka-dotted table. "I'll bring the drinks."

The woman's staring up at Ga'Rek, her mouth wide open.

"This is Ga'Rek," I tell her. "He's an orc, and he's my friend, and I'm a witch, and you are too. I assume that's why you're here, hmm? Your abilities just began manifesting?" I make the questions as gentle as possible, because she's as skittish as can be.

Rain pelts the windows, and Ga'Rek ambles back over as she stares at us, and then the plate of food in front of her.

He sets a plate piled high with ham sandwiches at the neighboring table, giving us space and the illusion of privacy while also being an arm's length away.

It's incredible how he does that, makes himself seem harmless and comfortable, despite his intimidating size and bulk. A little sigh comes out of me, and I tear my eyes away from him to focus back on the newcomer.

"Let's start with the easy part," I say, taking one of the fried potatoes laden in cheddar and popping it in my mouth. My eyes widen, and when I glance over at Ga'Rek, he's grinning widely at me.

It's delicious. Salty with the sharp bite of green onion and the rich, sweet flavor of bacon.

It's nothing like what I normally serve here, but I can't deny the fact this would be an instant winner.

"I knew you'd like it," he says in a low voice.

I squeeze my thighs together surreptitiously under the table.

"The easy part?" the trembling baby witch in front of me asks, her food still untouched.

"What's your name?" I ask her, wanting to put her at ease. "That's the easiest question I know." She swallows, her throat bobbing, and I nudge the plate closer to her. "Eat. That will help."

"Will it make them go away?" she whispers, her eyes huge.

I shake my head, so impossibly sad for her. I'm not one-hundred percent sure of the powers she's manifested so late, but I have a sneaking suspicion she's a seer, and not in the traditional sense.

A shadow seer, one who can converse with those who have departed this mortal plane.

"It won't make them go away," I tell her, and I suppress a shiver as I feel my mother's hand against the nape of my neck again.

Ga'Rek's watching me curiously, steadily eating sandwich after sandwich.

"It won't make them go away," I repeat, reaching out my hand and covering the other witch's with mine. "But it will help you control your gift. What's your name?" I ask again.

"Violet. Violet Islish." She blinks, looking just over my shoulder, where I'm fairly certain my mother's shade is hovering.

"Don't be afraid," I tell her, squeezing her hand before letting go. "The shades are nothing to be scared of. They're here to guide you. You don't come from… a family of witches, do you?"

She shakes her head no. The paper around the sandwich crinkles as she grabs half, barely audible over the sound of the rain on the glass windows.

It blows now in nearly horizontal sheets against the front of the store, the storm winds howling around the second story.

Ga'Rek glances at me and we both eat quietly, listening to the sounds of the violent autumn storm from our snug corner of The Pixie's Perch.

And waiting for our new friend Violet to feel safe enough to share her story with us.

Impulsively, I reach across to where Ga'Rek's hand rests on his table, and I cover it with mine.

I can't help but grin at the thought, because my hand doesn't even come close to covering his. It's a dab of pale skin against a sea of green, and I'm smiling at the contrast in sizes as I glance up at his face, heartened by the simple touch.

His mouth hangs open, his green throat bobbing as he swallows.

Air whooshes out of my lungs in embarrassment.

Trying to hold Ga'Rek's hand was not my brightest move, and shame dapples my chest and neck with flames of red.

Until he turns his hand over, grasping at mine the moment I begin to pull away.

We're staring at each other, that heat of shame climbing into my cheeks and turning into a different kind of heat entirely, when Violet begins to speak.

CHAPTER FOUR

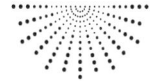

GA'REK

She's sought my touch not once, not twice, but now thrice.

Her dainty hand rests tentatively inside mine, so small and delicate that I'm afraid to move for accidentally hurting her. This hand that has only known violence and is calloused from years of holding a sword now holds something so precious I feel as though my heart might burst from the simple joy of it.

It takes me a moment to realize the scared woman has begun to speak, because I can't stop watching the way her hand sits inside mine.

"It started a few months ago," she says, her voice quailing. Her dark brown eyes flit between us and some spot just over Piper's shoulder.

A chill breeze brushes across the nape of my neck, and I rub one hand over it absentmindedly.

"It's okay, Violet," Piper says, her voice calm and strong.

A generous heart beats under her ribcage, and I narrow my

eyes. She's a study in contrasts: her ability to care so deeply for others and expect the least in return is baffling. She doesn't like that she needs help, doesn't expect it, doesn't want it—and then is embarrassed when I offer to ease her burdens.

And yet, she wants to carry everyone else's.

"Tell us. You'll feel better. Here," she pushes the steaming mug of tea towards the other woman, who picks it up with trembling hands. "It's charmed to help soothe the soul. I assume you know we're mostly witches and magical creatures here in Wild Oak Woods." Her voice is calm, steady, and the woman sips from the mug, then nods.

"That's—that's why I'm here. I thought you could help."

"We can help," Piper tells her, and I'm struck again by how easily she offers something she will not take.

I squeeze her hand reflexively, though, loving the fact that I might just be part of the 'we' she's promising. Helping is something I'm unused to, sure, though Caelan needed a fair bit over the years. Kieran, too, of course, the Unseelie prince the entire reason Caelan and I ended up in Wild Oak Woods at all.

Perhaps I'm better at helping than I think.

Perhaps I just need to convince Piper I'm the one she should count on.

"We can help," I agree, watching Violet swallow a huge chunk of sandwich.

"I went to the inn at the edge of town, but the owner, he said that they're renovating before a festival and the few rooms they have available are already let." Her voice breaks on the last word. She takes another bite of her sandwich, her cheeks full as can be as she stares down at the ham-and-brie in her hands.

Piper glances up at me, her brow furrowed, and I know without a doubt what she's going to offer.

I need to beat her to it.

"I have a spare—"

"You can have my room," I interrupt her, my voice booming

louder than the storm outside. "I have a room at that inn. I'll tell Caelan, he's the one tied to—I mean, he runs the place."

"No, I couldn't possibly," Violet starts, then claps a hand over her full mouth. Her eyes are huge and pleading, but it's not her I'm trying to help, not really.

Because this is an extremely selfish move on my part, and will put me exactly where I want to be.

"She can stay in my guest bed—"

"I'll stay in your guest bedroom," I tell Piper, grinning at her. At her, and at myself, because I can't deny that I'm very pleased by my own quick thinking. "Violet will be more comfortable in her own room, and then I have a much shorter trip to work in the early mornings, right, Piper? Plus, you've been so worried about this festival, and now I'll be around all the time to help with that."

Piper's pretty pink mouth is wide open as she stares at me, her cheeks rosy. She clears her throat, and I watch the smooth column of it tense.

I want to lick a stripe up it, scent her skin and put my ear to it as she begs for me to take her.

Like the former blood sport champion of the Unseelie Court, however, I control myself.

I've already made the opening ploy for Piper's attentions, by inserting myself into her guest room. Then she will accept my help for the autumn festival, and from there we will—

"I don't want to put anyone out," the newcomer says nervously.

"Don't be ridiculous," Piper tells her easily. "I love having people stay with me, and as much as it pains me to admit it, I need the help Ga'Rek is offering."

"I could help too," Violet says. "I mean, I am... all over the place right now, but you're being so kind, the least I can do is help with your festival."

"We will take all the help we can get," I tell her, and Piper makes a small noise of dismay. I arch an eyebrow at her, daring her to disagree.

She doesn't though. Instead, she rolls her eyes towards the brass and glass pendants hanging from the ceiling and sighs in defeat. "He's right again. I do need help, but we won't demand too much. The best person I can think of to help you would be Nerissa, for your type of magic."

"You're not... you're not afraid of me? Of... the fact I can see dead people?" Violet's eyes brim with tears.

"I've killed enough in my time that I would have to be a fool to be afraid of the dead," I tell her with a laugh.

She turns to me, blanching, and Piper pinches the bridge of her nose.

"What Ga'Rek means to say is that there is nothing to fear of the dead. It might not feel like it now, but this is a gift. Being afraid of death is normal, of course, but it isn't evil, or bad. It simply... is." She shrugs a shoulder. "It is part of the balance of life, and like all magic, seeing those on the other side of the veil only turns dark if that is your intention."

"I don't want to hurt anyone," Violet says, her fingers trembling as she reaches for the tea again.

I scratch my chin, because I'm not sure I would have the same reaction were I able to communicate with the dead. Not that I'm searching out people to hurt, not by any means, but I would surely have someone keep an eye on the Dark Queen for Caelan, Kieran, and me.

"I'll take you to Nerissa's as soon as the storm dies down," Piper says. She peers over her shoulder, at where the rain has slowed to a sleepy drizzle, though the wind still makes the old building groan and creak. "She's a spellsmith, and she'll help you start getting sorted out." Piper brightens. "Oh, and then you'll get a familiar once your powers have settled a bit, and you can join our book club, and you're just going to love it here. I'll send over some things for your room at the inn, too."

I smile fondly at her, because she's babbling and excited and biting off more than she has time for yet again, so eager to assist everyone that she comes in contact with.

I've never met anyone as kind-hearted as this brown-haired witch, who holds my hand.

My tusks scrape against my lower lip as I smile.

And I get to sleep in her guest room tonight, and until the new witch finds a permanent place to stay.

If I could reach my back to pat it, I certainly would.

CHAPTER FIVE

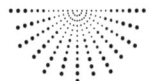

PIPER

Nerissa took to Violet immediately, her eyes as round as saucers as she instantly figured out what our new witch's powers were.

"They weren't kind to me either," she tells Violet, most of the melodrama she saves for the rest of us gone as she guides her to a navy blue chair next to her fire. "My family, the town I came from. You're in a good place now. We have a new coven, and we'll teach you everything you need to know. You're going to be okay," Nerissa practically croons.

Ears, Nerissa's huge wolf familiar, immediately lies on Violet's feet, whuffing gently as he breathes in all the interesting scents on her feet.

A dark blue rag rug spans the expanse of the honeyed wood floors in Nerissa's home, sprinkled with pale yellow dots that mimic the winter constellations that will shine brightly in the sky over Wild Oak Woods in a few months' time.

Violet takes in the cabin with wide eyes, and I cough gently as

I try to see it the way she must, for the first time.

It's the ideal witch's house, dark and snug with a stone fireplace that dominates the space. All manner of crystals and dried herbs line the mantel, along with brass and carved stone figurines that Nerissa uses for her spellwork. Unlike most of the rest of us Wild Oak Woods witches, Nerissa doesn't have a normal storefront or café, and she takes clients by consult, writing each bespoke spell especially for them.

As such, her front room is her storefront, and she's set it up to look exactly like her clients might expect. A repurposed brass bar cart full of clean glass jars sits to the side of a roll-top desk artfully littered with parchment and various colored inkpots. Exotic feathered quills march in neat rows along the back of the desk, each with a specific spell purpose.

The fire that crackles in the hearth isn't ordinary either, but sparks in purple and blue and smells like the winter's night that Nerissa draws so much power from in the long dark stretches of starlight.

"I have to get back; I'm so sorry," I say. "Violet, I promise I'll send some things up to your room at the inn. You are in good hands with Nerissa. I don't know exactly what you've been through, but you have a coven now, and while we—"

"We're going to take care of you," Nerissa finishes and makes a shooing motion at me.

I smile at her and reach down to scratch Ears on his wolfy head.

Violet nods, and Ears yawns as I stand up fully.

She doesn't believe us, not yet.

"I'll see you both soon," I say, lingering.

"Go on, you big worrier," Nerissa says. I scowl at her, then pull out the box of cookies I packaged up for her before Violet and I set out in the dreary rain for her house.

"Fine," I say tartly, but we both grin at each other before I leave.

I left Velvet waiting outside, because out of all the town's familiars, Ears understandably makes her the most nervous.

Overhead, the sky seems to exhale, a steely grey that whispers of the relentless change of seasons. I blow out a breath, grounding myself in this moment, and trying to practice the gratitude that my mother instilled in me as much as she instilled the perfect way to proof a sourdough loaf and how to fill an éclair with just the right amount of cream.

The air becomes too thick to breathe, my lungs aching with the need for oxygen.

I miss her so much.

I press a hand to my heart as Velvet leans against me, sensing the change in my emotions.

It's a funny thing, grief. Some days you hardly think of the ones you've loved and lost, smiling at a memory as it passes you by. Other days, it's like this, a choking vise of misery that makes it hard to breathe.

"She's not wholly gone," I tell Velvet, rubbing the soft white star on her forehead as my familiar looks at me with her chocolate brown eyes. "No one ever really is."

It's true. Even without the aid of Violet's visit, I know the ones I love live within me still. In memories, in the way I see my mother when I look in the mirror, in the way I can't help but try and assist everyone that stops by the store.

I inhale, and begin walking along the fairly empty cobblestone streets.

The wind whips along the corridor made by the buildings, the few passersby braving the rainy conditions hustling along with their cloaks drawn up tight against their faces.

Velvet clops along next to me, her little white tail twitching every so often. Lost in my thoughts, it isn't until I'm met with the sight of The Pixie's Perch bustling with end-of-day customers that I'm hit full in the face by the reminder that a certain handsome orc is going to be sharing my home with me tonight. And for the next few nights, at least, until Violet finds a place of her own.

My palms cover my face and my cheeks are ridiculously hot because all I can think about is how much I'd like to tell him to share my bed instead of the room next to it.

I'm a kitchen witch, and I certainly recognize a recipe for disaster when I write one.

Unfortunately, I'm not always bright enough to avoid putting quill to parchment.

MY BRAIN FEELS full with thoughts and plans for the autumn festival as Velvet and I amble along our street. The magic-lit street lamps come on earlier than usual.

I should bedeck them with some kind of decoration, I decide.

A smile brightens my face, because I know Willow is just the witch to decide on some sort of pretty fall florals to adorn each street lamp. Maybe Nerissa can enchant them to glow a different color for the festival, too.

That would really be something.

By the time I reach The Pixie's Perch, I'm in a much, much better mood, thoughts of all I have to accomplish racing through my head so fast it takes me a moment to realize how packed the café is.

My first instinct is one of delight, swallowed quickly by the panic of knowing that Ga'Rek must be swamped with orders.

I walk in, greeting the familiar faces and prepared to dive into work as soon as I've washed my hands, only to be taken aback.

Ga'Rek's head's thrown back in laughter, and Hank, a shaggy minotaur so tall his horns nearly scrape the ceiling, is laughing too, a box of pastries tucked under one arm.

The whole line's lit up with amusement, and I soak it in for a long second: the happy faces of customers who don't mind the wait, Ga'Rek a total natural behind the counter, and the smell of a bakery that's my home.

I'm nearly knocked off my feet by the sheer feeling of rightness.

When Ga'Rek locks eyes with me, that sparkling laugh of his still hanging in the air, it feels as magical as anything I've ever experienced.

A smile kicks up the corners of my mouth in automatic response, and his gaze heats as he continues to watch me from over the minotaur's shoulder.

I lift my chin, one eyebrow raised, a silent challenge he responds to by winking at me.

Winking! At me!

Well, how about that?

I purse my lips, making a beeline for the back of the store and the kitchen, trying to make sense of the whirlwind of emotions that threaten to overwhelm me.

Ga'Rek is staying the night with me.

I need to decide what, exactly, that means.

I need to decide what, exactly, I want to do about my no-longer-inconsequential feelings for him.

A clean tray in hand, I begin to carefully place chocolate croissants and almond tartlets in neat rows as I mull it over, wishing my pale skin didn't show all my heated emotions nearly immediately by burning up.

My mother used to tell me it was a good thing that I wore my emotions so close to the surface. I wonder what she would think about Ga'Rek.

It's almost as though I hear her soft murmur against my ear.

Life is too short, sweetling. Grab it with both hands and hold on for the ride.

I blow out a breath, knowing exactly what I should do.

There's only one thing for it.

I need to woo a warrior orc.

CHAPTER SIX

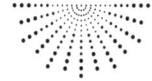

GA'REK

I barely get the chance to speak to Piper as the day winds down.

I'm intimately aware of her, though, the way she brushes past me to grab a pastry or a sandwich, the high-pitched musical patter of her speech with customers. The black tea and flour scent of her skin, always out of reach and tantalizingly close all at once.

By the time the crowd wears out, it's nearly full dark outside, thanks to the earlier evenings and the grey clouds hanging low over the town.

The contentment that rolls through me in spite of the exhaustion of having to deal with people for hours is a new and welcome feeling.

A job well done in the Underhill was met with the taste of copper in my mouth. Sore muscles if I was lucky, stitches and broken bones if I was not.

Any day that ended with me still on the right side of my

sword and not skewered by the business end of someone else's was a good day.

This is infinitely better, though I'm well aware of a surplus of physical energy I have left to burn at the end of the workday.

Although, I can think of a few ways to burn it off that are infinitely more pleasurable than anything I could have done in the Underhill…

And they all involve one pretty brunette witch.

I lock the front door after the last patron leaves, flipping over the sign to read 'closed.'

It's just us left in the shop. Not an unusual thing, but for me to still be here after we've cleaned and finished the day's work?

That is strange.

"Ah, so. I usually make dinner upstairs…" she says slowly. Piper winces, her nose wrinkling. "Make is sort of not, ah, reality, though. It's much less make and much more 'scavenge what's edible.' Then I drink a cup of chamomile tea from Lila's teashop, read or draw and go to sleep. Most nights." She clears her throat, her fingers working nervously at the apron tie she's double wrapped around her waist to keep it in place.

I want to unwrap her.

I want to untie the little bow she's made at the front and tease her as I take it off her body, then the clothes beneath.

My cock gets hard at the thought, and I adjust my own apron, too turned on to be embarrassed by the way my body is responding to every little twitch of her lips. Her gaze dips from my face to the small canvas cloth that does very little to cover my clothes, much less my body, and I stifle a groan.

I have to get myself under control.

Piper Paratee is more than just some idle lay to pass the time and enjoy in the moment.

I like her. I respect her. I want her.

I am not about to scare her off by taking that small, strong hand and wrapping it around the hard length of my cock. I'm not about to take her by her firm ass and hoist her onto one of the many tables in The Pixie's Perch so I can lap at the sweetness between her thighs.

I grit my teeth, my tusks digging into my lower lip at the force of my vivid daydreaming.

"I don't usually make dinner, you know?" she continues, waving her hand at the now empty and perfectly clean displays. "I'm usually too tired after baking all day to bother. But I could whip us up something—"

"I'll take care of you," I growl at her, and she blinks at the force of my words, like she's not sure what I mean by them.

By the Underhill, I'm not sure what I mean either. Now that we're alone, and the prospect of sleeping next to her with just a wall between us looms large in the future, I can barely control my need for this woman.

Maybe convincing the newly arrived witch to take my room at the inn was a mistake. Maybe sharing living quarters with this beautiful woman, this witch that I've wanted for weeks now, is a mistake.

Piper's tongue darts out as she licks her lower lip, and this time, I do groan.

Her eyes widen, and I know she's heard me.

My cock jumps at the idea of her listening to me moan her name, and a wet bead forms at the tip, dampening my trousers.

"I can take you out tonight, and you can tell me what you need me to do to make you come..."

She makes a startled sound, her lovely cheekbones turning rosy.

"To make you come to your senses about having me help you with the autumn festival," I quickly finish.

What the fuck has gotten into me? I'm about as smooth as a senile dragon's hide. All I can think about is making her come. Apparently so much so that the powers of language are starting to fail me.

"Honestly..." she bites her lip, and I have to look away from the way it changes color under the pressure. I want to watch her nipples do the same. Are they pink like her lips, or duskier brown? Are they small and perky or round and full?

I want to find out. The sooner the better.

I make myself inhale slowly, forcing thoughts of what are surely perfect breasts far from my mind. Food and help. That is what I am promising.

And if I do well enough, perhaps she will consider me a bedmate... or maybe even a real partner.

I've never been shy about what I want, and right now?

All I want is the kitchen witch blushing across the room at me.

"Or the Night Market?" she asks quietly. "Have you done that yet?"

"The Night Market?" I repeat. "Is that with the booths down in the square?"

"You haven't been yet?" Her face lights up with the question, and I want nothing less than to take her there immediately.

"It sounds perfect—"

"Unless you're too tired to go, which I would understand. I know I asked you to get here at the break of dawn—"

"I want to take—" I interrupt, but she forges onward, her face growing more stressed by the second.

"If you want to go to the Rowdy Wolf, that's fine too, I don't want to pressure you," she finishes.

I stare at her for a long moment, trying to decide how to tell her what's on my mind without terrifying her.

"I want to do what will make you happy, Piper," I finally tell her. I lean against the front door, crossing my arms, every fiber in my being wanting to cross to where she stands, stiff and unsure, and make her understand that. "I think the Night Market sounds like fun."

She brightens considerably, that light of excitement I've

learned to look for back in her eyes. "Really?" she asks, tilting her head.

"Really," I tell her.

"Oh," she slaps her forehead, and I take several steps towards her, wanting to kiss the spot she's hit, before I realize I'm already spiraling towards the point of no return with her. "I forgot. You'll probably need to go get your things from the inn first, right?"

I laugh out of confusion. "What things?"

"To sleep here. Your sleeping clothes, toiletries, that sort of thing."

"I sleep naked," I tell her, still slightly confused. "What sort of clothes do people normally wear?"

Her face turns red. Not the pretty rose I'm used to when she's flustered, but a full-on cherry shade of crimson that makes a laugh bark out of me in surprise.

Piper blinks, her mouth opening, then closing again.

"I didn't mean to upset you," I tell her slowly, loving the delicious way her throat moves as she swallows. "Or be coarse. I don't have things to collect. I wash my clothes every night, I sleep naked, and put them back on in the morning." I shrug a shoulder, and a muscle twitches in her temple.

Her gaze drifts down my body, and when she bites her lower lip again, I nearly jump over the counter and press her mouth against mine in a fierce kiss.

A delicious scent perfumes the air, and it's not the first time I've scented her desire… but it is the first time I'm fairly certain I've caused it.

CHAPTER SEVEN

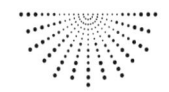

PIPER

I am doing probably the worst job ever at being alluring.

By the front door, Ga'Rek waits for me, a half-smile on his face, and I fervently wish I'd charmed some cookies with a teensy seduction spell earlier.

I brush my hair from my face, where it seems resolutely determined to fall, and untie my apron, hanging it on the peg to wash later.

Which, of course, makes me go hot all over at the mere thought of laundry. Laundry! All thanks to Ga'Rek's admission about how he sleeps.

Naked.

In the nude.

Just him and the sheets.

I loose a shaky exhalation, attempting to school my thoughts back into a productive place.

"There's a more secretive part of the Night Market, did you

know?" The question slips out before I can catch it. I cringe inwardly, well aware that he absolutely does not know, considering he hasn't been before.

"Secretive?" Ga'Rek repeats. He tilts his head, and the thick, glossy black bun on the back of his head moves with it.

I have been dying to touch his hair since the first week he worked here. He combs it out with his hands, tying it back with quick efficient movements I envy as much as I envy the luster of it.

"Piper?" he asks, and I startle, realizing I've been simply standing still, staring at him like a bump on a log.

"It's uh, it's not in the main square, but we can do that too," I say in a rush. Oh goddess, what if I've misread him entirely? What if wanting him has made me oblivious to signs that he's not into me the same way?

"I like the sound of being somewhere secret with you." There's a glint in his eye.

Hope and excitement fizz through my bloodstream, the heady combination a magic all their own.

"They have great food, this place," I tell him. "I'm a bit picky."

"I had no idea," he says, completely straight-faced, and we both stare at each other for a moment before bursting into laughter.

Beaming, I make my way from behind the counter, brushing careful hands over my favorite red skirt.

"Sorry I'm not dressed very fancy," I tell him. "I feel like I should be dressed up to go out with you."

He blinks, his long black lashes fluttering like soft moth wings. "I just told you I have one set of clothes I wash nightly. You are a goddess, and I will have the envy of every male in the entirety of Wild Oak Woods with you on my arm."

Pleasure at the compliment turns my knees positively wobbly, and I fluff out the asymmetrical hem of the skirt.

"Well," I tell him archly. "This *is* my favorite skirt."

"You look beautiful in it," he says, and the way he lingers over the word beautiful sends a fresh shiver of enjoyment down my spine. "I think you'd look lovely out of it, too."

My eyebrows shoot up, and I let out a delicate cough. If he keeps this up, I'm not going to make it to dinner. I'm going to rip his one shirt off and see just what's going on under there.

"I mean to say," he clears his throat, his cheeks turning that adorable deep green. "You are perfect in everything."

"Mmmhmm." I nudge him playfully in the ribs, and he laughs. "I see how it is."

At least, I really hope that's how it is, because goodness gracious, I like him.

I want him to think I'm pretty. I want him to mean all the nice things he's saying.

"You're very handsome, you know," I tell him, then look sideways, embarrassed at my sudden admission. "I'm not as good at this as you are."

Oh, goddess, I want to dissolve into a blob on the floor. Why did I have to make it awkward?

When I glance back up, cowardly, he's staring at me with intense concentration. He leans down until our faces are a mere inch apart.

I have to remember to breathe.

"What, exactly, do you mean by this?"

"I, uh, I—"

My bravery flees as quickly as it came.

"If you mean that you… want more than just a friendship with me, Piper, then you don't even have to try to be good at it. I'm not sure I could be wrapped any more around your finger than I already am." The words are low and fervent, and a hot feeling that has nothing to do with shame and everything to do with desire floods me.

He straightens up, leaving me to process that, and without warning, puts his hand against my back.

By. The. *Moon*.

His hand is huge, something I knew, obviously, because it matches the rest of him. I still wasn't prepared for the way it almost spans the width of my waist, his thumb curling around one side.

I want to ask him so badly what he means by me having him wrapped around my finger, but I also don't want to be off-putting or needy or too much or any of the other things men I've been involved with have told me.

The question flutters around the back of my head, though, from the moment I make sure Velvet is still snoozing in her spot by the door, and the whole time we walk down to the square.

Ga'Rek is quiet too, and when I glance up at him, trying to gauge his mood, he looks singularly… anxious, which is a look I haven't seen on his face since the first day he came to work for me.

I frown, confused. "Do you not like being around others? Is it too much?" I blurt.

The Night Market is hectic, it's true, the usually sleepy Wild Oak Woods downtown square turned into a bustling destination spot twice a week. Merchants from all over the region travel to sell their wares, setting up stalls with brightly colored canopies. Vendors who live here are present too, several mainstays being the enchanted ice vendors who produce melt-proof ice and fruit syrup-drenched desserts.

Those who flock to the market are a mix of Wild Oak Woods residents and those who live in the Elder Woods, and it's typically a feast for all the senses.

I could see why an Orc raised in the Underhill by the Unseelie fae might be overwhelmed.

Impulsively, I wrap my arm around his waist, or do my best approximation of it, because he's built like a primeval tree.

He huffs a laugh, his breath warming the top of my head.

"No, I'm not anxious around crowds. If I'm anxious, it's because I want to impress you."

My heart skips a beat.

"Quick-sewn bespoke clothes! Silks and cottons! Leather trousers!" a vendor yells. "A pretty dress for a pretty girl!" I glance sidelong at the cart, which is indeed laden with beautiful fabrics and sparkling notions: crystal buttons and brass fasteners, metallic trim and vibrant tassels.

Ga'Rek and I come to a halt as I stare.

I love clothes.

I don't get much opportunity to dress nicely. Most of my things are made with the utilitarian aspects of baking and work in mind. Thick linen skirts, like the red one I'm wearing now, cut in interesting patterns with serviceable blouses are my mainstay.

The midnight blue dress hanging from the top of the vendor's opened cart, however, is a tulle and velvet confection straight out of my dreams. Silver thread sparkles in the lantern light, wound into constellations amongst the airy tulle.

I step closer, transfixed by it.

"Elven made, that one," the vendor tells me. "Excellent taste."

"It's beautiful."

"It's a wrap-style too, wouldn't take much work at all to fit it to your specific measurements. We could have it worked up for you in an hour at most."

"Oh, thank you, that's really impressive..." I shake my head no, my hand falling away from where I've reached for the stunning garment. "I don't have anywhere to wear something like this, though. I'd buy it if I did," I tell the seamstress.

Spun midnight—that's what it looks like. Wearable night sky.

"Fabric like that doesn't come around very often," she says, and even though I know she's trying to sell me the dress, there's a kernel of truth in her words. "Elven-wrought fabric is rare."

"I need some things," Ga'Rek's voice booms out.

He pulls me back towards him, his touch gentle, and I go willingly, loving the way he doesn't seem to want to stop touching me, even though we're in public now.

Possessive, but in a way I really like. Affectionate, not overbearing.

And he's taken the shopkeeper's focus off me and the beautiful dress. I heave a little sigh, relieved, because the people pleaser in me wants to purchase the dress. To be fair, so does the part of me that wishes I had the kind of life that dress would require… but I very much do not.

Another woman approaches as Ga'Rek rattles off what he needs to the family of tailors, and she stares up at the dress with the same wishfulness I feel so deep inside.

"I'm going to go wander around," I tell Ga'Rek, because the thought of someone else buying that gorgeous garment makes me feel slightly sad.

He smiles down at me, and before I can process what's happening, he drops a casual kiss on the top of my head. His tusks bump against my scalp, and I grin up at him, flustered and thrilled at the public display of affection.

"I'll be at the stationery vendor," I tell him, slightly breathless.

"I'll find you," he says, his eyes positively devouring. It's the same look he gets before he tries one of my new recipes, and I have to say, it is not so bad to be looked at like that.

Not at all.

Whew. I try not to fan my face, and when I glance back over my shoulder at him, he's watching me walk away.

I might put a little extra swing in my step as I continue on my way to the vendor I need.

"There you are," Wren, one of my covenmates, appears in the crowd, waving a hand at me. Her long, wavy blonde hair is tied back in a pretty side braid, and her fox familiar darts between her legs as she steps towards me.

"I feel like I haven't seen you in ages," she says.

"It's been three days," I say with a laugh.

"Exactly. Ages," she agrees.

Fenn the fox stands up on his hind legs, and he makes his weird little fox noises as I scratch behind his ears.

"Where's Velvet?" Wren asks.

"She was napping, so I left her behind the counter. Deer security," I say with a dramatic sigh.

Wren snorts a laugh.

"Where's Caelan?" I ask.

"He's at the inn, he said he'd meet me here in a while. There's a new witch in town, did you hear?"

"I did. I sent her to him." My nose wrinkles as I realize the implications of that. "Ga'Rek said he'd give up his room—I didn't cause Caelan to have to work more, did I?"

Caelan, an Unseelie fae, waltzed into our lives with Ga'Rek and another fae several weeks ago and promptly set his sights on Wren. The two of them hit it off immediately, and they've been adorable to watch, despite our initial misgivings about the Unseelie fae.

"No, of course not, don't worry about that. He's happy to have a willing victim for the new hospitality measures he's implementing," Wren tells me in a conspiratorial voice.

"Wha—what?" Anxiety makes my stomach churn. "I thought he was getting ready for the autumn festival visitors. What do you mean, victim? He's not going to be up to any Unseelie tricks, right?' The words burst out of me, my good mood gone in a second. "He promised me he was going to help."

Wren glances down at me, alarmed. "That was a joke. He's excited to have an actual guest stay so he can dry run things like laundry service and the menu and get feedback from someone besides his oldest friends."

"Oh," I say, my shoulders slumping in relief and sudden exhaustion. "Okay."

"Piper, you still haven't told me what you need me to do for the festival," Wren says in a chiding voice.

"You've been so busy with work, and I know how stressed you were about getting the store solvent." Wren owns the store next door to mine, a jewelry store full of bespoke and custom-enchanted pieces. She's incredibly talented and finally seems to be overcoming a streak of very bad luck.

"Piper, you can't just pretend like it's all fine. We know you need help. We want to help with this."

"What I need right now," I say, a bit icily, "is some parchment and ink."

I brush past her, making a beeline for the stall stuffed full of paper and parchment and quills and ink. The merchant who runs it has a shop in town too, but I hardly ever have time to run over there during the hours we're both open.

Wren jostles my elbow as I reach for a deep emerald pot of ink, and I sigh, immediately regretting my defensive words.

"I'm sorry," I tell her, my fingers clamped around the ink pot.

"Don't be. Just tell us what to do."

"Caelan is already doing so much with the inn—"

She waves a hand at me. "Not me and him, us, the coven, us. We all want this festival to be incredible. We want to help, but we don't know what you need help with, or what you've already planned, or if you have a plan at all. We are happy to step in however you need." She stares at me, crossing her arms over her chest. "And if you need us to simply step in and take over, we can do that too. Don't even try to 'I'm fine' your way out of this."

My mouth opens, then closes, and opens again.

"That's a winning impression of a fish if I ever saw one," a smooth male voice drawls, and sure enough, Caelan appears behind Wren, wrapping his arms tight around her and planting a kiss on her neck. "Have you convinced her to finally accept help?" he asks her.

Wren, the traitor, just raises her eyebrows at me.

I throw my hands up in surrender, almost managing to toss the ink pot in the air, too. "Fine. Yes. I need help."

"That wasn't so terrible, was it?" Caelan asks me.

I glare at him.

Wren just laughs, patting her wily Fae on his purple cheek. "Be nice," she tells him.

"That's so boring, though."

"Are you looking for trouble, friend?" Ga'Rek's voice is a rumble behind me, and before I can react, he's also wrapping me in a backwards hug, his hand on my stomach sending butterflies reeling through me.

Oh, I could get used to this.

"Well, well, well!" Caelan says, a wicked grin on his handsome face.

Not nearly as handsome as Ga'Rek—too sharply beautiful, like broken glass.

Where Ga'Rek is all pleasant angles and rugged features, Caelan looks like he'll cut you from the inside out.

But Wren is happy with him, glowing, in fact, so I've pushed aside my own misgivings about the trickster fae for her.

He's not terrible either... not really. Just mischievous to a fault.

They're both staring at Ga'Rek and me with matching bewildered expressions, but Wren surprises me by recovering first. "Well. I suppose that settles the question of where he's sleeping tonight," she says to Caelan.

I blush.

Ga'Rek takes a step back, though, and my heart sinks.

"Piper has generously offered her spare room to me."

"That is *exceedingly* boring," Caelan tells him.

Wren's cheeks suck in like she's biting them, and from the way she won't look me in the eyes, I can tell she's trying not to laugh at her idiot of a fae lover.

"Ga'Rek is my friend," I say, my voice too thin and high and reedy to pass off as anything but as suddenly anxious as I am.

"And he is my friend too, little cookie witch," Caelan says, voice full of disdain. "It's clear that he's interested in cream filling of another sort, so you better hope your little éclair is sturdy enough to take it."

"Caelan," Wren whispers, scandalized.

"Enough," Ga'Rek's voice cracks like a whip, attracting the attention of everyone in the vicinity.

The poor shopkeeper who's been standing by, wringing her hands as our group monopolized the space, looks about ready to burst into tears.

"I'll take two of the green ink pots, a navy, a set of cold-pressed parchment, and three of the pheasant quills, please," I tell her, now dead set on ignoring Caelan completely.

She stammers a reply and begins packaging everything up. "Could I interest you in the seeded floral papers? They're new—"

"Yes," I tell her emphatically, also ignoring the way Ga'Rek is downright glowering at Caelan. "I would love a set of those."

"And we have a new pearlescent pink ink, it's charmed to allure all your admirers..."

"YES," I bark at the woman, "I WILL TAKE THE SEX INK."

The crowd goes a bit silent, conversation dropping before picking back up.

My ears are red now.

I can feel them.

"Well, I'll, uh, you know what? I'll swing by tomorrow to check on you. And we'll have a coven meeting tomorrow night. The coven will delegate any tasks you have left for the autumn festival." Wren's eyes are wide, her lips pulled away from her teeth in a cringe.

My molars grind so loudly I wouldn't be surprised if everyone could hear them.

"I will be there too," Ga'Rek rumbles in a no-nonsense voice. "Piper needs help and we will make sure she gets it."

"What an exceptional friend," Caelan says in an airy voice. "Certainly extremely normal for the Dark Queen's former assassin orc to volunteer to put on a festival. He is very qualified, you should know."

The shopkeep shoves a parcel into my hands, and I stare up at Caelan, who's grinning like the fiend he is.

"He's good at everything he does," I tell Caelan, forcing myself to be agreeable.

Wren sighs. "Don't encourage him—"

"Yes, good at rearranging people's guts," Caelan continues. "He is wonderful with bodies."

"Fuck off, Caelan," Ga'Rek tells him.

I blink, my mouth dropping at the unexpected expletive as much as the brutal shift in his tone.

Caelan simply laughs though.

Wren glances between his cackling face and mine, and shakes her head. "See you tomorrow, Piper."

Ga'Rek doesn't bother with niceties.

He doesn't even bother with my hand, or my waist.

Nope.

He picks me straight up, like I'm a parcel all on my own, and walks me from the awkward situation practically tucked under his shoulder.

I can't say I'm mad about it, either.

CHAPTER EIGHT

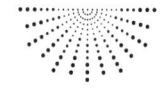

PIPER

"Um," I finally manage, both amused and gratified by the way Ga'Rek's literally lifted me out of an awkward situation.

We're garnering some strange looks, and I can't totally blame everyone for their interest.

Ga'Rek's expression is thunderous, and it's thunderous... on my behalf.

Besides, he's still holding me up.

One arm's locked tight around my thighs, my upper body squished into his.

"You know, I did always wonder what it would be like to see above a crowd," I tell him nonchalantly. "Do you know where I wanted to take you tonight?"

At that, he stops completely.

His brow furrows in consternation, and he looks from the crowd parting before him up to me.

I raise my eyebrows expectantly.

"No," he finally admits, his voice grinding out the word.

Finally, his arm loosens, and he sets me down. A hand goes to his hair, and he rakes his fingers through it.

My lips purse. "It's not far, but you're welcome to tote me around if you'd like. I could get used to seeing the tops of everyone's heads for a change."

As soon as the words leave my lips, I wonder if I'll regret them.

If the laid-back Ga'Rek I've come to know and like was just an illusion, waiting for the moment to pull the rug out from under me.

That possibility flickers before my eyes, and then he tips back his head and laughs, a booming sound that has people scattering faster than before from around us.

"I will carry you if you so desire, kal'aki ne," he says, amusement dancing in his eyes.

Much better than the ire that was there just moments ago.

We'll need to talk about that, I think.

"I am happy to walk, but if you need me to be your security doll to carry around, that's fine too."

He laughs again, this time quieter, more sly, and holds out his big hand.

I place mine in his, and tug him gently towards the alley of my favorite Night Market-only restaurant.

"There's nothing back there," Ga'Rek says, a bit uneasily.

I throw him a grin over one shoulder and walk faster.

The illusion blocking the alley shimmers, the dingy cobblestones turned gleaming as we pass through the spell. Ten tables line the alley, a family laughing at one as they eat, a couple cuddled up and talking in sweet whispers at a two-seater.

A server in a pretty dress smiles at me, nodding at an empty two-seater in the corner.

Ga'Rek's tall enough that he has to crouch to avoid hitting his head on the many glowing lanterns strung between the stone buildings. They illuminate the space with a warm, romantic glow, and the scent of heavily spiced meat weighs on the air, making my mouth water.

"I would never have known this was here," he says, clearly impressed.

"Aren't you glad you have me, then?" I ask, attempting levity after the weirdness with Caelan.

He doesn't laugh again, but fixes his intense gaze on my face. "Yes. I have never been so glad to have someone in my entire life."

My breath catches at that, and a warm, floaty happiness settles in my chest.

I squeeze his hand, at least, the portion of it I can hold, and lead him to the table the server indicated.

A thick, cream-colored tablecloth with a subtle rose pattern covers the table, and I smooth my palms over it in appreciation as I sit.

"This is here… only during the Night Market?"

Gleeful, I tuck a lock of hair behind my ear. "It's only here once a month during the Night Market."

His thick, dark eyebrows rise in surprise. "And the illusion?"

"Only on restaurant nights," I confirm, loving the way he leans in like we're telling secrets. The table creaks under his weight.

"Good evening, Piper, and you're Ga'Rek, right?" The family matriarch's standing next to our table, and I smile at her, placing one hand over Ga'Rek's in a sign of companionship.

I want him to like this place as much as I do.

"That's right," Ga'Rek says, slightly stiff. One hand goes to his waist, clenching around something that's not there before it falls in his lap.

"I've heard so much about you from Piper and Wren both. Caelan swings by to say hello too, sometimes. I'm Malia, by the way. Do you want to hear what we've made tonight, or have it be a surprise?" She smiles warmly at us both, her brown skin luminescent in the light of the lanterns.

Ga'Rek visibly relaxes, leaning back in his chair.

"I'd like to hear about it," I tell her. I love hearing about how other chefs work, especially Malia, who has an entirely different skillset than I do.

"Oh good," she claps her hands in excitement, and I share a grin with Ga'Rek across the table. "Today we have a selection of slow-roasted meats. Spice-rubbed pork, brined turkey, and there's even a side of beef. There's a hearty potato and carrot soup, loaded with salt-pork, cheese, and green onions on top, and then we have a selection of charred seasonal vegetables and some of the last summer peppers from the garden. We also have a board of early autumn fruits and cheeses we will start you off with, to whet your appetite," she pauses for breath, then looks straight at me.

"What?" I ask instantly.

"Now I'm nervous," Malia tells me with a laugh. "Because the best baker in the country is sitting here, and I'm about to tell her about my chocolate cream pie."

"Malia, you can do no wrong in the kitchen, and I've never found chocolate cream pie I didn't love." I beam at her, delighted by the praise and turning slightly pink from it, too.

She blows out a breath, shoving her hands into her apron pockets. "You'll have to tell me if it's not quite right." I open my mouth to argue with her, but she holds up a hand, cutting me off. "No, I mean it. I want your honest opinion."

I incline my head, amused, gratified, and slightly embarrassed at her insistence.

"Do you want wine?" she asks.

"Tea for me, please. Early day tomorrow," I tell her.

"Of course. And you?" she asks Ga'Rek, beaming at him with genuine kindness.

"I'll have whatever you think will be best with the feast you just described." His tusks glint in the lantern light.

"Oh, yes, I like a male that lets the chef decide," she tells him, then winks at me.

I laugh, and she scurries off to help another customer, her black curls bouncing as she goes.

"She's very kind," Ga'Rek says amiably.

Malia's daughter, no older than seven or eight, swings by, gingerly placing an earthenware pitcher of water on the table, along with several thick pillar candles.

She stares at Ga'Rek for a long moment, a serious crinkle in her forehead. "I've never seen an orc in real life," she tells him soberly.

He grins at her, and she tilts her head, considering him.

"Well, what do you think? Am I as scary as all the stories?"

"No-ope." She pops the last syllable. "You're too pretty to be scary."

With that, she skips off.

I bite my cheeks to keep from laughing, though I can hardly disagree with the child. A simple spell lights the candles, and I watch the flames flicker for a brief moment before looking back at Ga'Rek.

He looks slightly shell-shocked, and a moment later, another older child runs out to deliver the tray of fruit.

I bite my cheeks to keep from talking until she's out of earshot.

"I take it no one has ever told you you're too pretty to be scary?" I ask, doing my very best not to burst into a fresh round of laughter.

His huge green hand rubs his jawline, only succeeding in drawing attention to all that handsomeness.

"Most of the Unseelie treated me little better than their demon dog pets. Children didn't look twice at me in the Underhill. Can't say anyone there ever called me that."

"Oh." I wince. "I'm sorry. I didn't mean to make you uncomfortable."

He leans back in his chair, good humor still on his face. "Do you think I'm handsome?"

"Yes," I tell him instantly, then I cough, nearly fumbling the pitcher as I fill a glass just to give my hands something to do.

"You do?" he asks, and when I glance back up at him, I nearly upend my glass and spill it everywhere.

There's a predatory light in his eye, the kind that makes you want to freeze or run. The kind that promises if I tried to run, he'd catch me.

It doesn't freeze me at all. There's no ice in my veins.

The look in his eyes turns me molten all over, instead.

"I do," I finally manage to force out, and then, boldly, I slowly smile at him.

"Piper," he says, and there's a hint of pleading in the way he says my name. "I thought you said we were only friends. That's what you told Wren."

Oh. My nose wrinkles, and he breathes out heavily, leaning his arms on the top of the table, which groans under his bulk.

"We... are friends," I say hesitantly.

"But?" he asks, leaning further forward. There's a hint of desperation and the predator lurking in his eyes still, but I don't lean away.

I meet him where he is. "But," I summon all my bravery and forge ahead. "I've heard that friends make the best lovers."

A groan rumbles out of him, and I stare deep into his eyes, making up my mind once and for all. I want Ga'Rek. I want him as a friend, and I want him in my bed, and I want to know what it feels like to be touched by someone that looks at me like I'm precious.

"Piper, I'm not... I'm afraid I might hurt you." His eyes shutter for a moment, vulnerability making him look younger, softer, even.

"Well, we can figure that out." It comes out much more eager than I meant it too, but it makes him laugh.

"Soup and vegetables," Malia sings out, holding a steaming platter that her daughter helps her unload onto our table.

We both sit back and I bite my lip, excited and nervous and suddenly not hungry at all.

That is, until I take a deep breath and inhale the incredible aroma of the soup.

Ga'Rek has a huge portion in front of him, absolutely massive next to mine, and he stares between our bowls and the platter of vegetables as Malia watches.

"I do not wish to put you out with this large of a serving," he says quietly.

"That's part of the restaurant. No one here will go hungry. We size our portions based on how hungry the eater is. You are an orc, and you will eat like one under our roof." She glances up at the stars starting to wink in the gloaming night. "At least, under our lanterns."

He blinks, absorbing this. "Thank you," he finally says.

"Enjoy," she tells him, then winks at me again, ushering her daughter over to the next table.

"Did you think I would take you somewhere you would leave with a huge appetite still? You know minotaurs eat quite a bit too, right?" I laugh, tilting my head at the minotaur eating sedately with his family, their table piled high.

"I assumed if I were still hungry I could make a sandwich or four in The Pixie's Perch," he says slowly.

He dips the carved wooden spoon into the thick broth, the cheese melting across the top, with the kind of care I've become used to seeing from him in the kitchen every morning.

Usually, utensils look so small in his hands, but here? They're the right size.

"I could buy some tools that are larger for the café," I muse. "Are you having trouble using them?"

He raises an eyebrow before popping the spoon, perfectly

loaded with cheese and green onions and fried pork fat, into his mouth.

Ga'Rek's eyes flutter shut, and I beam, because I know that look.

That's the look of someone who has found complete bliss in their food, and Malia's one-night-a-month restaurant is one of the few places I eat with pure enjoyment, her cooking so good that my analytical chef's brain turns off the moment it hits my tongue.

"No," he finally answers, his green throat bobbing as he swallows. "I will not allow you to spend money on things that you cannot use."

"But you work with me. I don't want you to be uncomfortable using my things—"

"No," he says, shaking his head. "If I weren't able to use your things, I would let you know."

"Ga'Rek—" I start, but he shoots me a look so sincere that I simply close my mouth.

I'll just have to watch him more closely. If there's something he is struggling with, I'll fix it. Easy as that.

Cheese melts around my spoon as I dip into the thick potato and carrot broth, the green onions wilting from the steam where they float on top. It's so good—hearty and perfectly seasoned and everything autumn soup should be.

I love Malia's cooking.

"How does it work?" he asks abruptly.

"The soup?" I blink up at him, confused.

"The magic. Your magic," he clarifies. "I grew up with the fae. You utter charms and incantations as part of your recipes, but then you lit the candles here with no spell. The witch, Violet, who came by today, she didn't have to do anything to use hers."

"Ah." I take another bite of soup, then another, considering how to answer. "Magic is… everywhere. It's in everything."

He raises his eyebrows. "I don't understand."

My mouth twists to the side. "I'm trying—it's hard to explain something that's like breathing." I squint at a creamy lantern overhead. "You know you need to breathe, you understand the basic mechanics of it, right? But if you tried to explain exactly what your body does with the air…" I shrug.

He nods, looking intrigued.

Ga'Rek is an excellent listener. I really like that about him.

"Magic is like that," I continue slowly, trying to think back to the basics I picked up along with walking as a very, very small child. "It's in us, in witches. Sometimes, it's best channeled with a spell, like when I'm baking. Sometimes, with small tasks like lighting the candles, it's about will and intention. Every witch is inclined towards a specific discipline, usually something that crops up from family to family. Like Wren, she's called towards elements of the earth, gems and gold and silver. My magic is focused on feelings, which I channel into the food I make."

"The fae… they never used spells. Not that I saw."

"That's because they are more magic than most. Mostly magic, even."

He takes another bite of soup, swallowing slowly as he thinks it over.

Very serious, very adorable.

His mouth twists to the side as he studies my face, considering what I've tried to tell him.

I would like to kiss it.

Blushing, I quickly avert my gaze and take another bite of soup, then sample the platter of still steaming roast vegetables Malia brought out. The platter is a cracked deep blue glaze, and I'm reminded yet again of the starry blue dress I passed up at the tailor's cart.

What must it have been like to grow up without seeing the night sky change with the seasons?

"How did you end up with the Unseelie fae?" I blurt. It's something I've wondered for a long time about Ga'Rek. Orcs are fierce, yes, but they keep to themselves for the most part, in tight-knit communities mostly deep in the mountains, away from places like Wild Oak Woods and the larger cities along the coastline.

"Caelan took me from my parents when I was seven or eight."

"He did *what?*" I screech, my spoon falling with a clatter into my empty soup bowl.

Flustered, my mouth opens and closes, but Ga'Rek just barks out a loud laugh.

"He saved me, my sweetling," Ga'Rek says, his hand closing over mine, warm and comforting. "My parents were orcs, yes, and I'd like to think they loved me, but they..." He shakes his head, sorrow creeping into his beautiful eyes. "They were not good parents. They did not like being parents. They left me on my own for weeks at a time while they went hunting together. They drank ether—that's a grain alcohol that will burn the lining off your insides—until I was terrified they would never wake up."

"Oh goddess, Ga'Rek, I'm so sorry."

"Sweetling, it is long, long in the past. And it is not your hurt to apologize for."

My eyes well with tears all the same at the thought of a baby version of the lovely male across from me, fending for himself for weeks at a time.

"There was a bird I cared for—it was hurt, and I nursed it back to health. I was certain my parents would kill and eat it if they found it, so I stowed it deep in the forest away from where my parents liked to hunt, and I cared for it for many weeks while they were gone."

I twine my fingers through his, horrified for poor small Ga'Rek. Of course he took care of a defenseless animal.

"The bird was one of the many fae spies back then," he tells me, a humorless smile on his face as his thumb rubs lightly over the back of my hand. "One day, I went to take my bird a handful of berries and bugs I'd found, and it was gone. In its place was

Caelan, who told me he was going to take care of me the way I deserved, the way I did for the bird."

My chest positively aches.

"I went back, once. I don't know how much time had passed, because time here and time in the Underhill passes differently. My parents never even bothered to look for me." His eyes grow distant, looking slightly above and beyond my head. "I know, because I sent that bird I'd taken care of to look."

My hand goes to my heart. "Ga'Rek," I murmur.

"Caelan tells everyone he stole me," the orc says in a low voice. "And maybe he did. But what he really did, what he would hardly ever admit, is that he saved me, the same way I saved that bird."

I am at a total loss for words, so I just squeeze his big hand.

"Don't be sad, sweetling." His other hand reaches across the table, wiping a tear off my cheekbone I didn't know had fallen. "It was so long ago."

"Hurts like that don't just go away," I tell him. "I... thank you for telling me that. Thank you for trusting me with that piece of you."

"I would trust you with all my pieces, and all the parts that are still whole, Piper."

In that moment, I decide I'm not going to wait for him to kiss me.

I reach out, tentative, one hand on his cheek. His skin is much rougher than mine, beginning bristles of a coarse beard rasping against my palm.

His eyes pin me, and for a moment, I can hardly breathe, terrified to move—before I remember that this is Ga'Rek. This is my orc.

Then I'm moving, standing and leaning over the table, until our faces are barely a breath apart.

His gaze drops to my lips, and desire shoots up through my back, lightning hot and fast.

I move as he does, and our mouths meet. A huge hand brackets the back of my neck, possessive and needy. His tusks are strange, unusual, but not in a bad way—nothing about him could be bad.

I lick his lower lip, wanting more, wanting it now when—

"Ahem," Malia coughs.

We break apart, and I plonk back in my seat like a bag of flour.

She gives me a highly amused look, sweeping away the bowls onto a platter held by an older child, and then replacing them with dishes full of piping hot spiced meats.

I can't even bring myself to look at Ga'Rek.

Not because I'm embarrassed, but because I'm afraid if he looks at my lips like that again, I'll knock everything off the table and jump on him right here in public.

That would really get everyone talking.

As Malia sets down an array of ceramic pots filled with different sauces, I keep trying not to look at him.

"Enjoy, you two," Malia says, then flounces off with a knowing glance.

"This is delicious," Ga'Rek growls.

I snort, because he hasn't wasted any time, digging into the meat eagerly. It's somewhat awe-inspiring, actually, the way he's already downed enough meat for three meals of my own.

"Have I not been feeding you enough at work?" I ask, suddenly concerned with how much he's able to put away.

"Of course you have, Piper. But I'm not about to let any of this go to waste."

I shrug, my eyes narrowing, because I'm not sure if he's telling the truth or not.

However, he has a point about the meat.

A wicked smile turns the corners of my mouth up.

I don't want to let it go to waste, either.

CHAPTER NINE

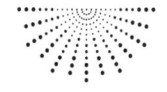

GA'REK

It's the best night I can remember.

Piper and I talk long into the evening, the only evidence left of the incredible food the scraps on our plates and the fullness in my stomach.

We walk back to her home above The Pixie's Perch hand-in-hand, contentedness wrapped snug around me.

Piper unlocks the back door to the kitchen and Velvet appears, wagging her tuft of a tail and stretching in greeting.

"Hi baby deer," Piper coos, and wordlessly, I go to refresh her water bowl.

Bending over, I pour fresh water in her bowl, and Velvet nudges at my hand in thanks. When I stand up, Piper's watching me, a soft smile on her face.

"Thank you," she says. "You didn't have to do that."

"Sweetling," I growl, something in me snapping at the way she's always helping others, never wanting anyone to help her. My feet carry me to her, and her eyes go wide as she steps against the back door. I put one hand at her waist, the other over her head, and lean in until our noses are nearly touching. "When are you going to realize I want to do things for you, Piper Paratee? When are you going to realize that I want to take care of you? When will you let me?"

She doesn't answer, not at first, just blinking rapidly.

When her small, soft palm caresses my jawline, I blow out a breath, my self-control nearly sapped. I want this woman. I want every last bit of her sweetness, want to give her pleasure until she's weak from it.

I want to show her that I see her, in all the ways. It's been a few weeks of letting myself admire her from afar, of watching her kind heart at work, softening to all the things she does for everyone else.

It's been a few weeks, but falling for her has taken no time at all.

She tilts her chin up, and I'm holding my breath, waiting for her to close the gap, knowing if she kisses me now, my self-control is going to be on a short leash. Her other hand goes to my chest for balance as she rises onto the balls of her feet. I bend down, curving to meet her where she is.

Her lips are impossibly soft as they brush against mine, and that's all it takes.

The need for her that's been building finally crests and there's no resisting her anymore.

My hand tightens around her waist, and when she sighs into my mouth, I lap at her bottom lip. She opens her mouth for me, and I groan as her small pink tongue chases after mine.

I'm on fire. My cock aches in my trousers and precum begins to drip, eager to be deep inside her.

"Piper." Her name is a fervent whisper, a plea in the dim light of the shop we've spent so much time together in.

"Upstairs?" she asks, pressing her forehead against my chest.

"Upstairs," I agree, and I swing her into my arms.

She lets out the most adorable squeak of a squeal I've ever heard, and I laugh, the sound of my happiness echoing in the small staircase. So small, in fact, that I have to crouch and walk us sideways up the flight and a half until we get to the small landing in front of the door to Piper's home.

I set her down gently, immediately missing the feel of her in my arms and against my body.

Piper tugs a key on a velvet ribbon out of her pocket, and the door to her home unlocks with a snick.

I'm beyond curious to see what her home looks like. The café and kitchen downstairs are so quintessentially her they're practically an extension of her personality, with their cozy nooks and mismatched chairs and pink and black and white accents.

She bites her lower lip and gives me a shy look, one arm wrapped around her waist like she feels the need to protect herself.

"It's nothing fancy." She begins to tuck that lock of hair that truly wants to escape the ribbon at the nape of her neck.

I get there first, brushing my thumb over her cheekbone as I push it behind her ear. It's just as satisfying as I've imagined it to be dozens of times.

"I've never had a home," I tell her. "Not really. Any place you touch, Piper, becomes magic. It has nothing to do with being a witch, and everything to do with who you are."

"Oh," she says on an exhalation. Her eyes darken, and she looks up at me from her lashes, her hand fisting in the fabric of my shirt as she pulls me inside her home.

I can't think of a better welcome.

CHAPTER TEN

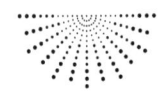

PIPER

Kissing Ga'Rek is my new favorite thing.

He keeps pulling away, and the look in his eyes is nothing short of worshipful. The thick length of his tusks are strange as they press against my mouth, but his kisses are so sweet that it doesn't matter at all.

I kick the door closed, and he reaches behind himself to lock it.

Once it clicks into place, I simply decide to lose my mind completely.

I jump, and he laughs, catching me under the ass as I wrap my legs around his thick waist, my skirt riding up around my hips. He's so strong—there's literally not one bone in my body that's worried about being too much for him in any way.

I slide myself up slightly, and we both groan as his cock rubs against my groin.

He breaks off the kiss and looks into my eyes. "Kal'aki ne, what you do to me." He shakes his head.

"Is that a bad thing?" I'm already breathless and, I'm willing to bet, wet for him, too.

"No. Never." His gaze darts between my eyes, like he doesn't know where to look, and I understand the feeling. I want to see all of him, touch all of him, all at once.

"Bedroom?" I ask.

"I won't be able to control myself if we do that. Maybe we should… take things slowly."

"Oh." It's sweet. Of course it is, sweet and so thoughtful, even though my body wants to do freaking anything but take it slow. "If that's what you want?" It comes out like a question.

"What I want, kal'aki ne, is to spread you out before me on the bed and taste your sweetness until you unravel from my tongue and tusks on your cunt."

All the breath whooshes out from me, and I stare up at him, practically salivating at the thought. "I like that option better. Can we do that option?"

He huffs a laugh, one hand coming up to cup my chin. "Oh, yes. We can do that. But there will be no coming back from it."

I blink, completely at a loss for what he means. "No coming back?"

"Mmhmm," he says seriously, nodding. "You'll be obsessed with me the moment I make you come."

I snort a laugh and cock an eyebrow. "Oh, is that right?"

"Yes, you will see. You will be addicted to my mouth, and then my orc cock."

I shake my head, still laughing. "Big words."

"It's a big cock."

"Well, then you better get to it," I tell him archly.

"Where is your bedroom, kal'aki ne? Or do you want me to feast on you right here, in your living room? Or should I put you in the window, spread you out on display, and let the whole street watch while I make you come?"

My eyes go wide at that, because that should absolutely not sound so alluring.

"You like that idea, don't you, kal'aki ne? I can scent it on you, your desire. You are full of surprises. But no," he shakes his head, his tongue darting out, licking his tusk. I want to chase it, do the same. I want to lick him all over. "I think tonight we will take it slow, keep this just between us, yes? We can play like that another time."

In one smooth, surprising motion, he lowers me onto the soft fur rug in front of my stone hearth. It's nearly dark up here, the coals still burning from this morning not nearly enough to cast more than a dim glow.

"Since you will not tell me where you want me to put you, I will put you right here."

I shiver, goosebumps scattering along the length of my skin.

"If you want me to stop, Piper, all you have to do is tell me, yes?"

"Yes," I whimper. "I've never wanted something as badly in my whole life. Please don't stop."

His laugh is as rough as his grip is gentle on my legs.

My back slides against the soft fur, my eyes wide as he kisses up my calf, his tusks scraping over the sensitive underside of my knee.

"You taste amazing already," he murmurs, eyes flashing in the low light. "Sweet as can be."

My boots come unlaced quickly under his deft fingers, and he takes them off, putting them on the hearth side by side before tugging off the thick socks underneath.

His fingers stroke up and down my calf, his gaze never leaving mine as he kisses along my legs. By the time he works his way up to my inner thigh, I'm panting, weak with desire.

The juxtaposition of his tender lips with the hardness of his tusks is like nothing I've ever experienced, and I find myself nearly keening as he rucks my skirt all the way up, exposing my underwear.

Ga'Rek's hands bracket my hips, pinning me to the lush rug.

His eyes are dilated completed, black swallowing the deep chocolate brown of his irises. He's watching me, completely still, and I can't stand the suspense.

I can't stand the suspense, yet I want more. Ga'Rek's drawing it out, teasing me, and it's so beyond wonderful that I don't want it to end.

He lowers his face to the apex of my thighs, and I moan as his hot breath warms the fabric of my underwear.

"So fucking sweet, kal'aki ne. I've wanted to taste you for days now. Wanted to know if you were as fucking incredible on my tongue as you smell." The words vibrate against my needy core.

I gasp, reaching for his hair, as he exhales hot air against me. He slides a hand down from my hip to between my legs, attempting to pull my underwear to the side... until he swears in frustration and simply rips in half.

"I'll buy you new ones," he says, and I laugh at the apologetic tone. "Or, you can just stop wearing them, so I can have my way with you any time I want."

I tilt my head back, laughing hard—until his mouth meets my flesh and my laughter abruptly cuts off with a moan.

My fingers tangle in the smooth slide of his thick black hair, my nails scraping against his scalp. His tongue teases for a long moment, only a hint of pressure, and his hum of appreciation makes me go tight all over.

I'm not wholly prepared for the feeling of his thick tusks parting me, making me completely accessible to the onslaught of his tongue.

I cry out, a wordless appeal for more, my body on fire, as he presses them against me, holding my pussy open. His tongue begins to lick in earnest, patient strokes that leave me shaking and needy for more.

He grunts in approval, and I brace myself against him. My chest heaves as he licks a slow circle around the bud of my pleasure.

"Ga'Rek, please, right there." My toes curl into the rug and he redoubles his efforts, licking and sucking at it until I'm practically crying with how close I am to the peak of pleasure. His hand moves up, teasing my folds, until he thrusts one finger inside me.

"So fucking tight. Tight and perfect and so, so sweet. This will be it for me," he groans, and I writhe underneath his ministrations, loving the praise, loving the way he makes me feel.

He adds another finger, and then, when he sucks my clit, he curls the pad of one into my body, finding a spot I didn't even know existed as I cry out. Pleasure explodes from deep at the base of my spine, my entire body floating on a cloud of it.

Gently, he keeps licking, teasing, until I come down, slowly, so slowly, that burst of orgasm so strong that I have to remind myself to breathe.

I open my eyes, trying to catch my breath, and his fingers are working at the buttons on my skirt, carefully undoing each and letting it fall away from my body. He lifts my hips gently, pulling it off and folding it neatly beside my boots.

I sit up, moisture dripping from my thighs, so ready for him, and pull my blouse off, practically tearing the rest of my undergarments off in my hurry.

"I want more," I tell him, tackling him to the floor.

He huffs a laugh, his mouth wet from the pleasure he pulled out of me, and I settle my naked hips over his. He's huge. It should be daunting, should be slightly frightening, the girth and hard length of him, but I don't care.

I'm ready, and I want him to feel as good as he made me feel.

"You are beautiful," he tells me, his hands going to my breasts. They're small, and I've never been overly fond of them, but the way he touches them, weighs them, his calloused fingers rasping over my sensitive nipples—it makes me believe it when he tells me I'm perfect.

"I need you," I tell him, desperate again. "I want to return the favor," I add. "I want to make you feel good."

"Orc cum is not like what you are used to," he tells me, all hints of amusement vanishing from his face. "Do not start something if you are not certain about me."

"Start something?" I roll my eyes, and he grins up at me, pinching one nipple until I moan again. My hips grind against his cock, still trapped in his pants. "It's already started. We started this together, and now I want to finish you."

"Kal'aki ne, the only way I'm finishing is inside you." His voice is a low growl that sends fresh goosebumps shivering over my skin.

My eyes have adjusted to the dim light, and I could drink in the way he's looking at me forever.

"Show me," I say on an exhalation. I fumble at the bottom of his shirt, and he starts to rip at it.

"Stop." I laugh. "You only have one shirt, and mine won't fit. If you come to work in only an apron tomorrow, the customers might like it, but I would be extremely jealous."

"Maybe I want to see you all jealous," he murmurs, his touch tender on my cheek. "Maybe I want you to want me in front of them, to show everyone you're mine."

I lean down, unable to resist his touch and his words, sealing our lips with a kiss.

A kiss that grows more fervent. I taste my own pleasure on his tongue, and he seeks mine out, chasing it with his. A growl grows in his throat and I finally lean back, hot and bothered.

I tug his shirt up more, and we carefully, finally, get the soft fabric all the way off.

"See? No fabric harmed in the process," I tell him smugly.

"You liked it when I ripped yours off. It made you come even harder for me," he says.

I pretend like I ignore him, but I love it—I love the way he's talking to me.

I run my palms down the muscled swells of his chest, then down the thick ridges of his abs. "You are a work of art," I tell him.

He raises one eyebrow at me, then raises both arms, flexing.

My laugh bubbles out before I can stop it, and all I can think is that I've never laughed this much during sex, not with anyone, not ever.

"I don't think anyone's ever gotten me to orgasm first," I say out loud.

Embarrassed, I stare down at him, wide-eyed.

"Good," he says, that feral, predatory look in his eyes once again. "Then getting you addicted to my mouth and my cum will be no problem at all."

I inhale, pushing down another laugh, because what the hell is he on about? "Addicted to your cum?" I snort, unable to hold it back any longer. "I'm sorry to disappoint you, but I doubt that. I highly doubt that."

His eyes glitter. "That's because you've never had orc cum. I am not making light of this, kal'aki ne. One taste of my cum, and you'll be wrapped around my finger as much as I am yours."

I pause, turned out but also now, slightly trepidatious. "You mean… those old rumors—I thought that was just old wives' tales." Gossip and hearsay, fairytales for horny witches.

That's what I always thought, though I refrain from putting that to words.

"It excites you," he growls, thrusting his still-clad hips up, making us both take a shuddering breath. "I can smell how much you like the idea of it."

"I do," I admit, surprising myself.

"I want you too, kal'aki ne. Don't forget that once you've had a taste."

My fingers tremble as I continue lightly tracing them down

his stomach, which ripples under my touch. It takes me a moment to unbutton his pants, which are worn thin and in need of replacing.

He shudders as I tug them down, his fingers still playing at my nipples.

His legs are just as beautifully muscled as the rest of him, and I slide my hands over his thighs in appreciation of the thick green expanse.

But it's his cock that I'm staring at.

"You can take it, kal'aki ne." His voice is so deep now that I hardly recognize it. "I will always get you ready for it, always make sure you're ready for me to stretch you from the inside. But my cum, orc cum, it has properties. One taste, and you'll want more. Drink too much, and you'll never want anything else."

I moan as he squeezes my breast, my core tightening on nothing in pure excitement.

"But the main reason for the cum, kal'aki ne, is because it will ready you for me. It will make you ripe and perfect. You will want no male but me again."

I don't even bother thinking too hard about that promise.

The lighter green head of his cock bobs as I drop down on all fours. It's leaking already, copious amounts slicking the top of it with thick, pearly white strands.

He pulls my hair to the side, watching my face avidly as I lick my lips.

My tongue darts out again, lapping at the substance, my gaze trained on him.

Until the first taste hits me.

I moan, in shock and in wonder, at the delicious flavor.

It's thick, almost as much as a pastry filling, the perfect silken texture coating my mouth and tongue. Sweet, with just a hint of musk, and an almost citrus tang to it.

It's not a myth after all.

I scoot closer, pushing his legs apart, and I dip my head down again, taking as much of him into my mouth as I can manage.

Goddess, he wasn't lying or exaggerating.

It's the best thing I've ever tasted, and it leaves me hungry for not just more of it, but for his cock deep, deep inside me, filling me up.

I'm wetter than I've ever been in my life, my own fluids dripping down my thighs. He's so large there's no chance of his entire length fitting into my mouth, so I wrap one hand around the base of it, my fingers not even close to touching.

This particular act, oral sex, never appealed to me before this very moment, and when Ga'Rek looses another wild growl of a noise, I realize it's because of him.

The taste of him, yes, but him.

He makes me feel safe.

I take him deeper, nearly gagging myself as I suck. His cum is incredibly delicious, and I can't get enough. My breasts tingle, my nipples stiff as they've ever been, and I reach between my legs, needing to touch myself, needing to ride out this feeling.

"That's enough, kal'aki ne," he says hoarsely. "Too much too soon and you won't be able to function tomorrow."

I don't care about tomorrow.

I only care about making him come, his thick member pulsing in my mouth, making me feel powerful and so fucking close to coming again myself, my fingers making frenzied circles on my dripping clit as I work him.

"Piper," he says, and I don't stop.

"Fuck, kal'aki ne," he says. "I'm not going to cum anywhere else but your pretty pink cunt."

I still don't stop, because why would I? I'm already floating away in a blissful haze, close to coming again, loving the way he feels in my mouth, in my hands.

"My sweetheart, kal'aki ne, sweetling," he says, panting, and then he's pulling me off of him.

I let out a low whine of dismay, and then I'm on my back again.

He takes my calf and puts it over his shoulder, and before I can register my displeasure at having his cock anywhere but inside me—he slams into me.

"Oh, Ga'Rek." It's somewhere between a shout and a moan, and he nips at my breast, then my neck, as I adjust to the glorious sensation of him inside of me.

I begin to shake, his cock pulsing.

"This is right and good," he tells me. "Isn't it, kal'aki ne?"

"What does that mean?" I manage, finally some rational thought returning.

He pulls out slightly, my body fighting to hold onto him, my fingernails scrabbling at his powerful, thick ass as he plunges back in.

Ga'Rek leans close, his tusks brushing against my ear. "My sweet. My heart. Sweetling."

I arch my back, his hot seed beginning to fill me, the ache of the incredible pressure of his cock stretching me easing up. As the tension recedes, pleasure fills the place it's left, and I moan, grinding my hips against him.

"Fuck, Piper, you are... fuck," he moans, then grabs my other leg, holding both of my ankles with one hand.

He takes his time, and his snarl of pleasure, lip curled away from his tusks, makes me wild with delight.

I can hardly move, the assault from his cock and his hand keeping my legs and hips from seeking him out. Ga'Rek's in total control of my body, and as his other hand reaches between us, rubbing my clit, I don't think I'd want it any other way.

"Come for me. Milk my cock. Get all the cum you need," he growls.

I'm senseless, floating, words I don't understand but that somehow make perfect sense coming out of my mouth as he gently rubs my clit, his huge cock stretching me, filling me.

When I come, pleasure making me shake all over, he follows quickly.

He comes, and comes, and comes, so much fluid it's hard to believe.

"There," he finally grunts, thrusting again. "Now you will come again, and milk even more from me."

I stare up at him, my mouth wide open, and then it hits me all at once—another massive climax, thanks to the properties of orc cum he said I'd be addicted to.

As I come down, slowly, exhausted, tired, wrought out, I have only one thought.

He was definitely, absolutely right.

There's no way I'm going back to another male after this.

CHAPTER ELEVEN

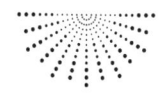

GA'REK

What I told her is only half true.

She will be addicted to me, to these moments—but I'm already addicted to her.

Her soft sighs, the fragrance and taste of her delectable cunt. The way her body ripples around my cock.

The way her pretty blue eyes stare up at me in wonder and pleasure, the ruby red of her lips, swollen from giving me pleasure.

I hold her close, nuzzling the top of her head, and even that slightly sweaty musk of her just cements her grip on me even more.

She's still pulsing around me, and I keep coming, the flow of it making her riper, her body opening up even more to me. Piper makes tiny noises of pleasure, mewling like a kitten, as she comes again, this time more gently, her whole body shaking with exhaustion.

Finally, I pull away from her, this meeting of our bodies coming to an end, but my bliss—our bliss—only beginning.

My seed flows from her, and I hold her legs wide, watching it with a possessive mania that surprises me with its strength.

"Look how good you are, my cum spilling out of you." I run a finger through her sex, and she cries out as I stroke her precious bundle of nerves. Some primal part of me wants to shove all of it back inside her, to fill her up with it until she's thick with my child.

That's not me, though, and the thought jars me out of my post-sex haze.

"I should have asked you this before," I say in a hushed voice. "But are you, could you—"

"I drink a contraceptive tea."

Relief and disappointment war within me, but she smiles up at me, sleepy-eyed and beautiful, and my warring thoughts finally wane.

"That's good," I make myself say.

She stretches out, her arms going long over her head, her mouth opening wide in a jaw-cracking yawn.

"Come," I tell her, scooping her up in my arms and holding her close.

"I think I've done that about as much as I can," she says, slightly weakly.

My dick bobs, still searching for her cunt. I could fuck her until the wee hours before daylight, could continue to make her come, but she will want to work in the morning.

I know that about her, and knowing it gives me great satisfaction. Even though fucking her until she can barely move sounds like a fantastic way to spend the night, her being too tired and mad at herself for it tomorrow isn't worth it.

Her smiles are worth it.

Besides, I'll have tomorrow night to look forward to.

"I'm going to take care of you, sweetling," I tell her.

It takes me no time to decide which room is hers, but I open the third door in the hallway and deposit her in the huge footed copper tub. The bathroom is painted an earthy grey-green that appeals to me, reminding me of the forest. It's fairly dark, but my orc sight means I see just as well in the dim light as I do in the day.

"Shall I light the candles for you, Piper?" I ask, fiddling with one of the brass knobs until hot water comes out.

We did not have anything like that in the Underhill, and it's a luxury I'm not sure I'll ever be fully used to.

Smiling, Piper utters a quiet word, and the sconces on the wall flare to light, then settle into a gentle flicker that dances along her skin.

She's peaceful, quiet, and totally amenable to me washing every inch of her pretty body. Cum still leaks from between her legs, and I'm loath to clean it up, but I don't want her to be uncomfortable, so I gently wash her there, too, rinsing out the rag several times to do so.

"Do you want children, Ga'Rek?" she asks me, her voice heavy with sleep.

I blink, surprised by the question.

"I don't know," I tell her honestly. "I've never had the opportunity to think that a family could be for me." My throat constricts, and I attempt to swallow around the knot forming there.

"I understand. I'm sorry; I don't mean to pry—"

"You are not prying," I interrupt. "No, do not even think of apologizing."

She grows quiet, and I swipe the washcloth over the slope of her shoulders again. The bubbles from the vanilla-scented soap cling to her skin in a way that makes me envious of them.

"The orc mating urge is nothing to be trifled with—it's something I knew even as a child. Something my parents were able to teach me, if nothing else." I didn't expect the words to come out, didn't plan the admission in any way.

Water sloshes as her hand rises, her slim fingers wrapping around my wrist. "Ga'Rek."

Now that I'm talking now, though, now that I'm... feeling like this, like she's mine, I need to tell her; I *need* her to understand.

"My parents did not like each other. They were mated, yes, but their bodies chose each other. Their personalities were not... it was not good."

I fall silent, and she squeezes my wrist gently.

"We're not your parents, Ga'Rek. We were friends. We still are... but now, I suppose..." she trails off, her skin reddening on her chest, where her breasts bob at the surface of the soapy water.

"Now we're more, yes?" The question is low and dangerous, and that mating urge surfaces again, primal, feral, dangerous.

"We're more," she agrees quietly. "I choose you, too. And not just because," she clears her throat, half-turning in the tub to look at me. "Not just because of what we just did."

"You mean where you came so many times from my tongue and my cock you nearly blacked out?" I ask, arching an eyebrow mischievously. "That's what you mean, about what we just did?"

She blushes furiously, but lets out a small tinkle of a laugh. "Exactly. We are more than that, and if I pushed you faster than you wanted—"

I cut off her words with a fierce kiss, her sigh of happiness replacing the anxious line of questioning.

"You did not push me at all. I have liked you since the moment I walked into your magical café. I wanted you the second you invited me to come work for you. I knew I cared about you deeply the morning you ran to Wren's house bawling, upset about the duchess's visit."

She kisses me then, a gentle brush of her lips against mine. "We will take this one day at a time. We aren't your parents. My mother told me the secret to relationships." Her lips curl in a smile, and she rubs the tip of her dainty nose against mine.

"You know the secret to relationships?" I ask, astonished. "That's quite the secret."

Her smile grows, and she crooks a finger at me. "Come closer and I'll tell it to you."

I lean forward, intrigued and pleased with my little kitchen witch.

I like what she whispers in my ear so much that I slide one hand under the water and part her folds, caressing her until she comes again.

CHAPTER TWELVE

PIPER

We've been slammed all day.

I keep trying to sneak looks at Ga'Rek, but we're so busy with customers, he and I barely have time to do more than smile at each other across the store.

My feet hurt, I'm sore in places I didn't know I even had, but all of that pales in comparison to the bubbling happiness deep in my soul.

Ga'Rek held me all night. Every time I stirred, he would whisper in my ear and rub my back until I fell back asleep.

We got to sleep much, much later than I normally would, but I'm more well-rested today than I have been in a long time.

We both ate a lemon-curd tartlet for breakfast enchanted with an energy spell, but I'm not sure I would've needed it.

I only wish we could have cuddled in bed longer this morning, that we could have had a lazy breakfast snuggled up by the fire instead of getting right to work in the dark hours of morning.

The Pixie's Perch is close to closing, and there hasn't been much of a chance for either of us to do more than sneak a sandwich. But tonight...

The bell tinkles over the entry, and my hopes for tonight go up in smoke immediately. My entire coven has walked into the store, replacing the rush of customers with a familiarity I at once love and am annoyed with.

Only because I want to spend time with Ga'Rek.

The realization makes me warm again, and I grin up at them.

Wren bustles over and makes herself at home behind the counter, grabbing a sandwich and a pastry while she's at it.

"Forgot lunch again?" I ask her drily.

"I was busy. I've been so inspired lately." She's so enthusiastic that I can't even be annoyed with her presumptuousness. Besides, she's my friend. She knows I'd stuff food in her mouth if she asked me to. We both know it.

Nerissa leans against the countertop, dressed in her typical array of black and thick silver necklaces. Ears sits on his haunches outside the store, stoic until he glances back at his witch, his tongue lolling out.

Then there's Willow, our local apothecary and plant witch. She's more disheveled than usual, her red hair standing up with frizz, likely due to her standing over her cauldron all day or working in the heat of her greenhouse. Her owl familiar perches on the street light outside the shop, her feathered head swiveling around.

Ruby holds an enormous leatherbound book, her long-haired cat familiar already making himself at home in Velvet's bed behind the counter. She struggles to set the book on a recently cleaned table, and I raise an eyebrow at her very serious expression.

My nerves jangle.

"What's wrong?" I ask slowly. It's clear something is very wrong. I can't remember the last time all of us were able to show up in one place unannounced. Book club is different, and we're not always all there. Our coven meetings have been few and far between as we attempt to get the proper legal paperwork filed with the magic administrative branch to declare us the official Wild Oak Woods coven.

"Tell her," Ruby says, the directive aimed at Wren, who's still eating like she's starving.

I rub my forehead and make a mental note to send her a basket of food more often. Wren often gets so involved with her work she completely forgets to take care of herself. Caelan's helped, I'm sure of it, but if he's busy with his inn then maybe she needs me to help her—

"The Seelie queen stopped by," Wren says airily, interrupting my train of thoughts.

"What the *fuck*?" The question rockets out of me. "When? Just now?"

The last customer of the day looks up from his book, startled, and then collects himself before standing to walk out the door. His little hooves clip clop on the tile.

"Have a great day," I call after the silver-haired faun as he leaves.

"Er," Wren says, wringing her hands. "It might have been about a week ago now."

I wait until the door closes, then scramble over to it in an attempt to lock it.

Only for Kieran and Caelan to waltz right through it. I glare at them. I scowl at Wren, but she's not paying attention. I pinch the bridge of my nose.

Caelan scoops Wren up into a huge hug, kissing her thoroughly. She squeals as he twirls her around, then dips her and kisses her again.

Kieran stands awkwardly in the doorway, which I'm now holding open.

Willow very studiously ignores him, even though the lilac-hued Unseelie fae works with her now, same as Ga'Rek and me. Clearly, they don't have the same connection we do.

A permanently sour expression turns down his mouth, on what would otherwise be a very handsome face. I peer behind him, curious as to what the buzzing noise emanating from behind him is, only to gasp in surprise.

Wings. Full-on, iridescent wings.

Wow. They're gorgeous. And I had no idea they were there.

I didn't even know some of the fae had wings.

"Did the Seelie queen have wings?" I ask Wren. "Or did you forget to mention that, just like you forgot to tell me she," I cough delicately, "stopped by to see you?"

Caelan and Kieran both freeze, and Wren pales slightly.

"I wanted to tell you, but I got busy, thanks to the queen, actually, and you have been so busy too, and I just... I wasn't sure when the right time would be."

"The right time was as soon as it happened," Ruby interjects.

Ga'Rek finally walks into the main restaurant space, a cleaning rag in his hands.

"Did you know?" I ask him.

It's stupid, but the thought of him keeping something from me like the Seelie queen visiting another witch in Wild Oak Woods, especially Wren... hurts.

"I didn't know," he says quietly. "I would have told you, kal'aki ne."

The tension dissolves from my chest, and before I fully realize I'm moving, I'm at his side, nestling into his chest.

"Ahh, that is what this day has been missing," he says into the top of my head, his arms circling around me.

"Oh, let me guess," Caelan says in a sing-song voice. "You two fucked last night, and now you're in your orc mating frenzy? How predictable. I told you sleeping in her guest room would be boring."

"Caelan," Wren admonishes, sounding scandalized.

Embarrassment at his crude language makes me bury my face deeper into Ga'Rek's chest.

"Don't talk to her like that," he growls. There's more snap in his voice than I've ever heard.

The Pixie's Perch falls fully silent, thick with tension.

The rest of the coven shifts slightly away from where Ga'Rek and I stand, and I don't have to look at them to know they've moved into a defensive formation, something we haven't practiced but every witch learns as soon as they're able to wield magic.

"Apologies, Piper Paratee, kitchen witch," Caelan finally says, smoothly. "I am still getting used to these... mortal niceties."

"He means he's getting used to there being consequences for saying and doing whatever he wants." Wren sounds pissed.

I glance up, still clinging to Ga'Rek's side.

Caelan does appear contrite, but from the way Wren's glaring at him, I get the distinct impression she's not going to let it go that easily.

"I did not mean to... ah, embarrass you," Caelan tells me delicately, glancing quickly up at Ga'Rek and then away again.

I look up at him, too, curious what in my kind orc's face has Caelan looking like *that*—when I see it.

Ga'Rek's face is practically contorted with anger. His tusks are bared, his lip completely curled back from them. His forehead is furrowed, and his shoulders are tense.

"That's the mating urge," Kieran says, staring at Ga'Rek with clear fascination. Unlike Caelan and Ga'Rek, Kieran's rarely spoken in front of me. He has an urbane, precise diction that's nothing like the other two, but fits his polished appearance and sharp, pretty features. "I thought it was a myth."

"That's because you are a child and a fool," Caelan tells him.

Wren elbows him in the ribs. "Rude," she hisses.

Ruby covers her face, and Willow just stares at her feet, even quieter than usual.

"You are all acting like idiots," Nerissa finally pronounces drily. "There is clearly something afoot. First, Hash turning into a Seelie and binding Caelan, an Unseelie trickster, to the inn."

"He did not bind me," Caelan interrupts, annoyed.

"Yes, he did." Nerissa, despite being shorter than Caelan, manages to look down her nose at him. A neat trick, really. "Or would you prefer if I said he tricked you into running it? Hmm?"

Caelan glares at her.

"That's what I thought. Then the Seelie queen shows up and gives Wren a quest."

"It was not a quest, it was a commission—"

"Different word, same outcome." Nerissa waves a hand, dismissing Wren's summation. "You get a magic tiara for her, she has a magic tiara. Then, you have the prince of the Unseelie seeking refuge in Wild Oak Woods after being kicked out from the Underhill by the Dark Queen."

My mouth drops. "I'm sorry, what—"

"Prince?" Willow says, coming alive at last. Her red curls bounce along her voluptuous breasts as she swivels towards Kieran. "Prince? Unseelie prince?" She lets out a wobbly laugh. "Of course you are. That explains it all."

Willow takes a few steps back, shaking her head, and drops into chair, her head in her hands.

Ruby sighs, then throws her hands in the air. "We have a problem. Something is brewing between the two fae courts, and Wild Oak Woods seems to be the epicenter of whatever is happening."

"Epicenter sounds so dramatic," Caelan opines.

Ruby attempts to level him with a cutting look and he shrugs one shoulder, disinterested in any and all of her judgment. "The queen of the Seelie fae visited, but she's not the only one of royal blood expected here soon, right?"

"I should have said something sooner, I was just so excited to have her commission me, and then she spread the word about my shop, so I have been busy." Wren's face scrunches up as she talks, and she leans back on Caelan for support.

"It's all right, Wren," Willow interjects. "We know now, and I think we can all agree that we don't know what to make of it, or of… any of this, really. Let's focus on what we can control, and look for patterns in the mean time."

"Unless the patterns find us first," Nerissa mutters in an ominous tone.

A beat of silence passes by.

Ruby draws a deep breath. "The duchess is visiting next week, correct?"

I press a hand against my stomach, nauseous with anxiety all over again. "She is," I finally manage to confirm.

Ga'Rek's wide hand rubs gently between my shoulder blades, and I lean on him, comforted.

Oh. That's what everyone wants me to do.

Lean on them.

Lean on them, receive the support, and feel better.

It's so simple I nearly feel stupid.

"The duchess is coming next week," I repeat, my voice stronger.

Ga'Rek's hand stills on my back.

"She is coming next week." I take a step away from him, finding my own balance. "And we are going to put on the best autumn festival Wild Oak Woods has ever seen." I take a deep, shaky breath, meeting each person's eyes, one after another.

"I need help." My voice cracks on the last word. "And the fae, if they are planning something, we need to figure that out too, but—" I pause, pushing my hair out of my face. "But I need help with the festival, and we have one week to do it. Will you help me?"

Wren squeals, startling me, then wraps me in her arms. "About time you asked!"

"I knew you could do it," Nerissa says, smug.

"You're in charge of food, obviously," Ruby tells me. "Nerissa, you're in charge of assigning vendors places. I suggest we tap our Night Market vendors to come in for the weekend. I know a few bards, I've already sent word to them for entertainment. Willow, you can work on florals and decorations, right?" Ruby takes a breath, momentarily ceasing her rapid-fire allocations of jobs. "We will plan a tour of the shops in addition to the festival for the duchess and her retinue, and introduce her to all the best things our town has to offer, and we will cap her visit off with a feast and a dance with the bards. We can also plan a magical display as part of the entertainment." She nods to herself.

Nerissa cuts her gaze to me, her dark eyebrows arched and ruby lips pursed in surprise.

"A magical display will fulfill part of the coven formation guidelines too. We can introduce ourselves as a coven to the town and duchess all in one go. I'll ask her to sponsor our application, too." She rubs her hands together.

I blink, just as surprised by Ruby taking charge as Nerissa seems to be.

Willow is the first to talk. "And what of the other royalty we have in Wild Oak Woods? What's the protocol for dealing with... that?" She waves her hand at where Kieran stands, his arms crossed over his leanly muscled torso.

A strange look crosses his face, a fleeting look of desire and despair that catches me so off-guard and is gone so fast I think I must have imagined it, or misinterpreted it, at the very least.

"The protocol is we aren't going to do anything about it," Ga'Rek growls. "Kieran's status isn't relevant. There are enough other species here that Caelan and Kieran can blend in. We don't need to broadcast our location to any of the Underhill's spies that may want to report back to Her."

"Blend in..." An idea occurs to me, an idea that I can't put aside or dismiss now that it's popped into my head. "Blend in," I repeat, "or stand out. The party you want to throw as part of the festival," I nod at Ruby, "which I think is a great idea, by the way —what if we make it costumed? Then anyone who wants to come… who might be afraid of being seen, can blend in?"

Nerissa claps her hands together. "That is a great idea, and I have a costume I've been dying to wear."

"A costume party." Kieran grimaces as if that's the worst possible thing in the world.

"If you want to go," I tell him. "If not, then that's fine too. But that way you can attend without being as worried, right?"

Kieran looks to Caelan for guidance.

Caelan shrugs. "A magicked illusion is more likely to draw attention than a costume. If She's even looking for you at all."

Kieran's expression shutters, and I wonder how awful it must be for him—forced from his home, and not only that, but his own mother, the Dark Queen, the one to exile him from it.

I would be very, very, sad and upset if I were him.

"We would like for you all to come," I tell the fae, then glance back at Ga'Rek, who's quietly closed the space between us.

Something like satisfaction shimmers in Caelan's eyes, and he inclines his head at me.

"Wild Oak Woods is your home now too," I tell them, and I mean it.

"Let's get to work," Ruby says. "We plan the festival, and then we research the fae queens."

"We will leave you to it," Caelan drawls.

Wren sighs.

"Unless you want us to stay, of course, little witch." The trickster fae takes her hand in his, pressing his lips to her knuckles as the corners of her lips twitch in response. "I am, as ever, at your disposal."

Wren glances at me, asking if I need them to stay.

Ugh.

I need help, yes, but Ga'Rek probably misses his friends.

"I want you three to put your heads together and decide on a theme for the costume party," I tell them. "And," I draw the word out as inspiration strikes, "I want you all to work on finding a place and constructing a few platform stages, with lighting, for performers to use."

"We could use their input on the queens of the fae," Ruby says plaintively.

"If we can offer insight on the queens, we will. But," Caelan mimes locking his mouth shut, "we may not be able to give you information you want without attracting... Her spies."

Kieran rolls his eyes. "My mother is a cutthroat monster ruled by her desires and her lust for power. I am happy to shed any light necessary on her behavior, but I am sorry to say that I was the spare, and thus not included in any political machinations regarding this realm or the Seelie."

He inclines his head, his pale, silvery hair falling over his face. The only sign of his discomfort is the slight buzzing of his wings.

"Well, Kieran's always known exactly how to suck the fun from every situation," Caelan says with a frown. "But yes, that is the extent of it. The three of us might have been in court, but we were hardly a part of it in any meaningful way."

"She's vicious," Ga'Rek's voice rings out. "We are well rid of her and the court. And should she show up here, she will learn what it means to reap what you sow."

Caelan's devil-may-care expression hardens into something else entirely, something savage and ancient. "We will defend you, and this place, with our very lives. Threatening any of you is the last thing she would attempt."

Kieran's gaze lands on Willow, who resolutely stares at the floor.

"She is not one to underestimate," he adds, and there's a dark, foreboding quality to the pronouncement. "Farewell, witches of Wild Oak Woods."

His wings rustle as he turns and swaggers out the door.

My eyes narrow as I study the exiled fae prince, now lurking next to Nerissa's wolf familiar.

Willow sighs, folding her hands in her lap, gaze flitting to where he stands outside, framed in the red light from the setting sun, and back at her hands.

Ga'Rek strokes one hand down my cheek, distracting me completely from whatever it is that's bothering Willow. "I will be back later, yes, kal'aki ne?"

"I would like that," I tell him, and reach for his face.

His lips meet mine, and all I can think is that I can't wait for later.

Caelan and my orc follow Kieran out of The Pixie's Perch, and I exhale.

At least I have help now, from my coven, and from the unlikely three from the Underhill.

And so, with a heavy load of things to do weighing on me, I turn to my fellow witches and rub my palms together.

"Let's get started."

CHAPTER THIRTEEN

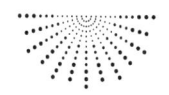

GA'REK

I doubt anyone else can tell how anxiety-riddled Caelan is right now. Kieran, perhaps, though the prince isn't known for being either empathetic or caring.

So I kiss my sweet witch goodbye with the promise of another night together hanging between us.

"Rowdy Wolf?" Kieran asks, glancing at the neighboring pub's already busy exterior.

"The inn," Caelan says in a clipped tone.

Kieran casts one forlorn look at the pub, but to his credit, he doesn't argue at all with Caelan's order.

We're quiet as we walk down the cobbled streets to the outskirts of Wild Oak Woods. The many citizens we pass greet us by name or with a smile, and it warms my heart to see evidence that the three of us, despite our status as newcomers, have been welcomed into this small hamlet.

"This is a good place," I rumble as Caelan's new inn comes

into view at the very end of the street. "I won't allow the Dark Queen to ruin Wild Oak Woods."

The inn, which seemed to be nearly crumbling only a few weeks ago, now soars up from the ground, delicate archways supported by fluted columns, a rainbow's array of stained glass coloring the windows, and a wraparound porch that's nothing like what was there.

Hash, the old innkeeper, besides turning out to be a Seelie, had a few tricks up his sleeve where his inn was concerned.

I frown.

"It *is* a good place." Kieran's voice rings out in agreement, unexpectedly. He's agitated, his wings rustling as we walk up the wildflower-lined path to the porch steps. "I won't let her ruin it."

Caelan shifts his gaze, and we share a surprised look.

It's not like Kieran to take a stand. On anything. Or anyone.

We reach the front door, and Caelan opens it. Out bounds Boner, the small dog Caelan inherited with the inn from old Hash. Unfortunate name aside, he's a good dog, though I can't say I like being licked by him.

"The timing is odd," Caelan says slowly, picking up the pup and scratching him behind the ears. "All of this," he says, jerking his head to indicate the inn.

It's no longer old and falling apart, the illusion so deftly woven over the place that my two fae companions hadn't even noticed. All that remains since Hash left is an old, beautiful building at the edge of the Ever Forest, well-preserved, luxurious —and nothing like the place we sought refuge in when we first arrived here.

I'm not magical, not like my two friends, and certainly not like Piper. Still, I lived in the Underhill long enough to recognize the tang of it on the air when I encounter it.

"Why is it here?" I ask.

Caelan sits down at the long wooden trestle table that dominates the large, cathedral-like room, steepling his long fingers before covering his face with them.

"It's the Ever Forest," Kieran says casually, leaning against the large desk designed to greet guests. His wings buzz ever so slightly. "I don't know why Caelan hasn't said that outright, but that's the reason."

Caelan's mouth pinches into a thin, irritated line. "We don't know that."

"This is a waypoint." Kieran continues like Caelan hasn't spoken.

"Waypoints are fiction. Myths." Caelan pinches the bridge of his nose. "This is just... a house."

"You are being reductive," Kieran counters. "You did not study at the Underhill Academy."

"Here we go again," I mutter, swallowing a laugh. I reach for my dagger, fully prepared to sharpen it and give my hands something to do while Kieran and Caelan argue, then I remember I no longer carry it at my hip. I don't need to.

"Kieran—" Caelan begins.

"No, I am right about this." Kieran gives Caelan a vicious, angry look I've never seen on the careful prince's face.

I have, however, seen that same look on his mother's face, right before she ripped a courtier's heart out with her bare hands.

My eyebrows rise, and I cross my arms over my chest.

Kieran's wings rise up, vibrating angrily behind him, and my heart begins to beat faster. Dread ices my veins.

I didn't think the prince had this in him, and I don't like the way he wears his mother's violence like a mantle.

One side of Caelan's mouth kicks up in a twisted grin, and when he glances around Kieran's wings at me, he smirks.

"Are you right about this?" he asks.

I rub my temples, because I know that look on Caelan's face.

He is goading the prince.

"I am right about this," Kieran hisses. He stabs a finger on the wide oak table for emphasis.

"Why do you care so much? These aren't your people. This isn't your town. You never gave one shit about what happened to anyone in the Underhill besides your own selfish hide."

The rage radiating from Kieran becomes palpable, chartreuse magic shimmering around him.

I don't know exactly what Caelan is attempting to do, but I know him well enough to recognize a trap when I see it. I take a step closer to the two powerful Unseelie, ready to step between them if the occasion calls for it.

"What, my young friend, are you willing to stake on being right about it?"

There it is.

That's a hook from a trickster fae if I've ever heard one.

"I would stake my life on being right. This town needs protecting, and this inn *is* a waypoint."

"You would protect it?" Caelan asks quickly, almost eagerly. "At all costs, even against your mother?"

Ah, fuck.

"Of fucking course I would, and you should too. Isn't the little silversmith witch your mate—"

Kieran's voice breaks off, and he raises his hand from the wooden table.

A drop of crimson blood shimmers on one lilac finger, and his wings lower, his shoulders sagging.

"Ah-ah, you don't get to be mad," Caelan tells him in a satisfied voice. "A little blood oath never hurt anyone."

"*Fuck* you, Caelan."

"So sorry to tell you that position's been filled, little prince." Caelan's eyes shimmer, fresh anger dancing in his eyes. "By the little silversmith witch, as you, yourself, just said. My mate. So forgive me for ensuring her safety through whatever means necessary."

Kieran doesn't reply, just glares at him for a long, tension-filled moment. "You didn't need to trick me into swearing a blood oath. You are my *friend*. I don't want you to hurt because something happens to your mate. I care about this place, too."

Caelan's smirk disappears, a frown in its place.

"I might be an Unseelie prince, Caelan, but I am not my mother. I am who I choose to be."

With that, Kieran storms off, his chartreuse magic sparking behind his wings as he goes.

A door slams so loud a moment later that it rattles the art on the walls.

"Well, that could have gone better," Caelan finally manages.

He even looks slightly embarrassed.

"Don't move," I tell him in a low, dangerous voice.

He freezes. "What?"

"I want to remember this moment forever." I put my hands up, bracketing his face like a frame. "The moment you finally felt bad about tricking someone into a deal."

He has the grace to let out a small laugh, then slumps, his face in his hands.

I cross the distance to sit across from him at the table.

A moment passes, viscous, as I wait for him to speak on whatever it is he's troubled by. This isn't like him. Not at all.

I can't remember one time when the wise-cracking fae wasn't able to deflect all sorts of horribleness with an ill-timed joke.

"What are you thinking?" I finally ask, cracking under the heavy silence.

"He's right," Caelan says slowly, and there's despair in his eyes when he finally drags his face away from his hands. "He's right. The inn is a waypoint. There is strong, thick, wild magic here. That's why, I think, none of us realized what Hash was up to when he disguised it. This place... it's full of secrets, and I am sure they are not all for me to find out. The witches, the coven, the Seelie queen's appearance—there is something headed towards Wild Oak Woods, and I do not know what it is."

His face is stricken, and I swallow hard at the unsettling sight of an emotion on Caelan that isn't pure chaotic glee.

"You think someone is guiding events? Our expulsion from the Underhill…" I pause, shaking my head in disbelief. "I'm just an orc. One stolen by a trickster fae, not even a proper orc."

Now his expression turns manic again, the Caelan I know and love. "Oh, not a proper orc? I suppose your Piper had some complaints then, did she? About your proper orc performance."

I stare at him with a hard face until he chuckles and glances away. "We all will have a role to play in whatever it is that's coming. But it's building, whatever it is."

"That's what they tell me too." A new voice pipes up, and when we both startle, glancing towards the west hallway, the newcomer witch is there.

Violet.

The dark circles under her eyes are still there, but there's a new-found strength shining in her eyes, too.

"Who told you what?" Caelan asks, confused.

"The dead," she says simply, shrugging one shoulder.

Caelan swivels back to me, his eyes wide. "Because that is an entirely normal thing to say."

I try not to laugh, for the sake of the willowy witch who I know must be scared out of her mind, yet was brave enough to traipse into the front room with an orc and an Unseelie and then eavesdrop on their private conversation.

"It is decidedly not normal," Violet says with a huge sigh. "And frankly, I am not sure how I feel about any of this. But the dead told me to come here, and now I am, and they whisper amongst themselves."

The hairs on the tops of my arms rise.

"They say too, something is coming. Something from the old

woods." Violet shrugs again. "I'm going to bed. I came to tell you both thank you for your kindness."

I incline my head automatically, the odd niceties of the violent fae court ingrained in me at this point.

"Well," I draw the word out long, stretching my legs out in front of me. "I don't know if that makes me feel better or worse," I say lightly.

It makes me feel much worse, and I decide I can't even be mad at Caelan for striking an unwilling blood oath with Kieran.

"The old woods," Caelan repeats, his brow furrowed. "The Elder Forest."

It clicks the moment he says it, and I very nearly smack myself in the face for not realizing it beforehand. "The Elder Forest."

Of course.

"Do you think the bookstore witch has anything on the Elder Forest?" Caelan asks me. "That rude one? With the cat?"

"I knew who you meant by bookstore witch, Caelan," I reprimand him. "You didn't need to add the rest. Her name is Ruby."

"Of course it is. Why would I call her Ruby when bookstore witch works just as well?"

Boner, curled up by the fire, lets out a noisy fart in his sleep, and we both wince.

"I'm not sure if I should reward him for that or check underneath him," Caelan confides.

"Can you please focus?" I'm used to Caelan's frequent digressions, but this is not the time. "What the hell can we expect from the Elder Forest? What is powerful enough to set all of these pieces in motion?"

His amusement at Boner's interruption fades, and he shakes his head. "I don't know. But I don't have a good feeling about it, not one bit."

I growl. "I don't like preparing for an enemy that I know nothing about."

"We have a powerful group of women on our side. We have an Unseelie prince, one who needs a few centuries of training still, but who's bleeding raw magic every time he gets upset. We have you, one of the strongest warrior orcs I've ever seen, though you're growing soft from filling pastries—"

"Caelan." His name's a warning.

He laughs. "We have me, whom you can always expect to have a few tricks up his sleeves. Then there's the Seelie queen, who has decided to get involved all on her own. I have a feeling destiny has brought us here, to Wild Oak Woods, to have some fun."

That manic glimmer returns to his eyes, and he smiles, the firelight dancing off his sharp Unseelie fangs. "Whatever is building, whatever storm is coming, it will have to get through us first."

I nod in agreement, because he's right. There is no way I won't fight for Piper, or for the future we could have together.

The witches on their own will be formidable, but together, with us by their side?

There will be a reckoning.

"Now, on to even more serious matters," Caelan says conspiratorially. "What terrible theme should we choose for this event? I was thinking we could have cats as the theme."

"Cats?" I echo, completely thrown by his sudden change in topic. "Why cats?"

"Why not?"

"I can think of a lot of reasons why not, Caelan. That suggestion makes no sense at all."

"Carrots," he says.

I stare at him. "A carrot-themed party. A carrot-themed party with dancing. Dancing carrots."

"Yes, you see the vision." He gestures expansively. "Orange décor. Carrots galore. Green headpieces."

"I do not see the vision," I tell him flatly.

"You are absolutely no fun." He sighs, then brightens. "Knife-themed. Everyone can dress as though they are being gutted."

"You are forbidden from deciding the theme," I tell him. "You are done."

"Death and dismemberment," he continues, ignoring me completely. "There are simply so many ways to have that happen. People's imaginations will go wild."

"I will tell Piper we've decided on a fall theme." I pinch the bridge of my nose.

"That is quite possibly the most boring option of all."

"It's a harvest festival."

"Oh yes, and everyone will be simply delighted by the redundancy of a fall-themed costume ball."

"If they were delighted by a death and dismemberment theme, we'd be right back in the Underhill," I mutter.

His face falls. "Ugh. I suppose you are right. That was a ghastly event."

I open my mouth, then close it. I don't even want to ask.

"We need to start constructing props and stages," I say, exhausted.

"Oh, that's no problem. None at all." His tone is so breezy and unconcerned that I fight the urge to flip the table on his ass.

"Oh? Have you suddenly become an expert craftsman?"

"No, but the minotaur brothers down the street are, and they owe me a favor." He gives me a sly look, and I narrow my eyes at his toothy grin.

"By the moon, Caelan, what did you do to the minotaurs?"

"Nothing," he says gleefully.

"Bullshit," I tell him.

"Precisely," he agrees. "It's not my fault that they simply have had terrible luck at finding work lately. Has nothing to do with the odor of manure that's pervading their shop."

I noisily exhale through my nostrils. You can take a trickster fae out of the Underhill, but you can't take the trickster out of the fae.

Typical.

"Well, I am sure they will be delighted to have the work, and I am sure I can talk them into a very steep discount for the good of the town. Maybe they can construct a giant carrot."

"No fucking carrots."

"I like carrots," he says.

"No."

"Potatoes?" he asks.

"What?"

"A giant potato. For the festival."

"Pumpkins," I enunciate slowly. "Pumpkins are a harvest vegetable."

"So blasé. So expected."

I stand up, the bench squeaking across the floor.

"Where are you going? We've not finished our planning."

"I'm going to see a minotaur about some pumpkins," I say evenly, unsurprised as Caelan trails behind me, holding back his laughter at himself.

At least he's his own best audience.

By the time I return to Piper's lovely apartment, she's half asleep in an armchair by the fire, so beautiful it makes my heart ache.

She glances up as the door closes behind me, and Velvet, who's sleeping by the fire, opens one eye before settling back in.

Fresh bread steams on the table, a teapot in a knit cozy set out next to a clean cup with a bowl of sugar cubes next to it. There's sliced honeyed ham on a platter with fresh vegetables, and I grin at the carrots, thinking of Caelan's absurd root vegetable fixation.

"Hi," she says tentatively, her voice husky with sleep, one slim hand reaching for me.

It's a scene of domestic bliss, one so unfamiliar and dreamy all at once it makes my heart ache.

"Kal'aki ne," I tell her, smiling wide, so happy I am afraid to think about it too hard, for fear it might slip away. "You are so beautiful."

She smiles wide at me, then yawns. "I made you some bread. I thought you might be hungry."

"Oh, I am hungry." The words rasp out of me. "But not for what's on the table."

A laugh bubbles out of her, her wide smile delighting me to no end. "Did you eat?"

Piper pauses, waiting for a response.

I shake my head, because, no, we did not.

"We got the minotaur builders to agree to make the props and things for the festival," I tell her. "We were busy."

"You need to eat," she says firmly.

I cock my head at her. "Will it make you happy?"

"If you eat? Yes."

"Fine." I nod in agreement. "But I have one condition."

Her eyebrows shoot up. "What's that?"

"You have to sit on my lap." I dive forward, grabbing her around the waist, and head for the table as she giggles, the sound music to my ears.

"You can't eat with me on your lap."

I pretend to ignore her sweet protests and grunt instead, pulling out one of her tiny chairs, slightly terrified I'm going to break it, but I sit down anyway.

"If my woman wants me to eat, then I will eat. You'll be surprised at all the things I can do at once," I tell her.

She slides down my chest, settling onto my lap, and I know the exact moment she realizes my cock is rock-hard for her, because she lets out a breathy moan that has me wanting to rip her clothes off immediately.

The anticipation, though, it keeps me from breaking my word

to her.

The longer I drag this out for us both, the more satisfying it will be.

So I hum under my breath in appreciation of her hot cunt, her perfume flooding the air, and I grab the loaf of bread, tearing into it.

"Ga'Rek," she laughs, her body further relaxing into mine. "I would have cut it for you."

"No, it's not safe for you to have cutlery in your hands right now."

"What are you talking about?"

Her laugh is the best thing I've ever heard.

"Holding a knife would be very dangerous to your health," I murmur against the soft skin of her ear. My hand moves from the lovely curve of her waist to the hem of her dress, and I tug it up as she moans, one hand curving around the nape of my neck, holding me close.

Fuck, this woman.

"Kal'aki ne," I tell her, breathing in her sweet scent. "You are wet for me already, aren't you? Dripping, hot, and ready."

She arches her back, sliding her right leg further over my thigh until it's dangling to my side.

Groaning, I drag my hand higher up, teasing my fingertips against her inner thighs, until I find the soft thatch of hair covering her perfect cunt.

"No undergarments, kal'aki ne?" My eyes squeeze shut, because fuck the bread, fuck the ham, I want this witch in my mouth right now, I want her to come all around me. "You are so ready for me."

"Take a bite," she says in a throaty voice. "Take care of yourself while you take care of me."

As if I could think of anything but making this woman come, right now, in my lap.

I tear off a huge hunk of bread with my teeth, managing to get crumbs all over her—which makes her laugh again, a sweet sound that cuts off into an even sweeter moan as I rub my fingers down her soaked cunt.

I don't want the fucking bread.

I don't want anything but her.

"Ah, fuck, I want you so bad."

"Eat," she admonishes, even as she writhes, chasing my touch.

Grumbling, I take another bite, basically swallow it whole, then set the stupid bread down as I plunge two fingers deep inside her.

She groans, her cunt so wet and welcoming I nearly spend in my pants at the feel of her.

"That's my Piper, that's my sweetheart," I tell her. "Take what you need."

"Need you," she says, her blunt teeth scraping along my collarbone.

I use my thumb to rub her, watching her eyes grow heavy-lidded as her hips arch into my touch. "You smell fucking amazing," I tell her in approval.

"Ga'Rek," she whines, and my cock jerks.

My other hand reaches under her blouse, freeing her breast. It takes me no time at all to find her nipple, and when I pinch it, hard, she cries out again.

"Are you going to come for me, Piper? Like this, in my lap?"

She moans, her eyes rolling back in her head, but she's still not there, not yet.

But she will be.

"Do you need more, Piper?"

She makes a sad whine as I take my hand off her breast, freeing my cock from my trousers. Her little fingernails dig into my skin where she holds the back of my head, her other hand braced on the forearm of the hand that's working her into a frenzy.

"Need you," she gasps. "I want it."

"You don't need it yet," I tell her, chuckling at her whine in response. "You're going to come like a good witch, right here, while I talk to you."

Her arousal thickens around me, intoxicating.

She's close now, and I think I know what's going to tip her over the edge.

"I'm going to fuck you at the festival, Piper. I'm going to let my cum drip down your legs, and you're going to wear my scent so everyone knows your mine. I'm going to take you into a corner, where anyone could see us, and I'm going to make you come right there in front of the whole town."

"Oh, goddess," she moans, and I jerk my hand over my cock, gritting my teeth as I barely keep myself from coming.

"You like that idea, don't you, kal'aki ne?"

She whimpers, nodding.

"Use your words."

"Yes, I like that."

I reward her by moving my hand from my aching cock back to her breast, and she jerks her hips forward at the increased sensation. "Tell me what you want me to do to you at the festival, Piper."

"I want you to fuck me where anyone could find us," she whispers. Her core tightens around my fingers pumping in and out of her, proving exactly how badly she wants it.

I grin, well-pleased, as precum pools around the base of my cock, leaking fast now.

"That's right, I know you do. I know you want everyone to know you're mine. You want them to know you belong to me. You want them to scent me all over your pretty cunt, don't you?"

She moans again, core so tight now that I'm dying to fuck her. "That's what I want, yes."

"Then that's what you'll get. Because I will always, always give you what you want." Overcome with desire, I release my hand from her, bringing my fingers to my mouth and licking her wetness off of them.

Before I realize what she's doing, Piper's slid off my lap onto the floor.

She looks up at me with a devilish smile and wraps her hand around my cock, her other hand massaging my balls.

"Fuck, Piper."

She's beautiful like this, and I don't think I will ever get tired of seeing the way she tries to take my cock into her lush mouth, her pink tongue licking up and down the green.

She sucks hard, and I stiffen at the overwhelming sensation.

"Is my big orc going to come?" she asks, fluttering her eyelashes before wrapping her lips around my cock again. "Do you want to come in my mouth?"

My hand goes to the back of her head, and she moans, the vibrations delicious on my sensitive member—and that's all it takes.

"Fuck, yes," I tell her. "Take it."

She moans again, the low hum killing me.

I come hard, jerking into her mouth as she sucks, and sucks, swallowing my spend.

When she finally pulls away, I'm panting, and she wipes her mouth off.

"I'm not done with you yet," she purrs.

Her clothes are on the floor in the blink of an eye, like the witchy goddess she is, and I tear off my shirt and pants in an attempt to match her speed.

"It's only fair if I'm naked too," I tell her seriously, and she laughs as she climbs onto my lap, straddling me.

My hands go to her breasts, her hips, overwhelmed by how gorgeous she is, how good she feels, how lucky I am. When she guides the thick head of my cock into her body, I know I'm home.

"I want you forever," I growl.

"Good," she pants, sliding me, inch by inch, into her. "Because you're right. I'm addicted to this."

She kisses me hard, and my hand wraps around her neck, possessive, the way an orc in a mating frenzy would—because that's what this is.

That's what she is.

"My mate," I rasp. "Kal'aki ne."

Her eyes are wide in surprise, and I thrust up, causing her to cry out as her small breasts bounce.

I curl forward, catching her nipple in my mouth and sucking it.

"Ga'Rek," she moans, fluttering all around my cock, her cunt so sloppy and wet for me that pride surges through me.

"You're mine, Piper, and you're going to wear my cum like a fucking brand, do you understand?"

For a second, worry sears through me that I've gone too far, said something she won't like.

"Please, please," she says.

"I want to fuck you hard, Piper. Say no and I'll hold back."

She looks up at me, her lovely eyes wide, breath-taking, and I'm so afraid she'll say no, so afraid I'll lose her it hurts.

CHAPTER FOURTEEN

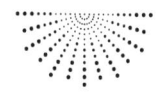

PIPER

"Harder," I whisper, staring into his brown eyes with complete trust.

His mate. He wants me, to be with me, forever. That's what mating means. I asked Ruby, and she summoned a book on orc customs from her store that I spent the whole night reading.

Still, he doesn't move, staring down at me like he's terrified.

"I want you to take me hard, my orc," I demand. "Take me like you mean it, mate."

That's what the book said orcs mated like. Demanding. Hard.

I took off my underwear as soon as I read it.

"Fuck, Piper."

He moves so quick I gasp. I slide out of him as he wrenches me around, then takes an arm and knocks everything off the table.

I can't find that I care. He shoves me onto the table in place of the table settings, and I moan as his hands grip my hips, pulling me close.

"I'm going to take you like the orc-mate you are," he growls.

One huge green hand spans the width of my wrists, and he pins them above my head, so tall that he barely has to stretch to do it. Like this, on my knees, I'm forced to have my ass up in the air, and he laughs, then blows a breath of cold air against my hot pussy.

"Oh, goddess," I moan.

Then he slowly presses into me, and I whimper again.

"Tell me if it's too much," he says roughly. "I'll be careful if I can, Piper."

"Fuck me harder," I grate out.

He swears, the slow rhythm he started turning jerky. Turning harder.

"Come inside me," I continue, getting wetter with every stroke of his cock. "I want to feel you so deep."

He slams into me at that, and we both groan, my toes curling.

I raise my hips up higher, encouraging him. "Show me I'm yours, Ga'Rek," I tell him, close to coming again.

And he does—releasing my hands, his arm curling around my hips until he finds my clit again, working me with his fingers as he rams into me.

When I come again, he does too.

This time, though, he doesn't take me to the bathroom. Doesn't clean it up, doesn't pull out.

No, he gingerly carries me into my bed—our bed.

We doze together for a few hours, and when I wake up with him hard inside me again, I'm more than ready for another round.

"We're taking the day off tomorrow," I tell him breathlessly.

"The week."

"The week?" I ask.

He slides out of me, and my back arches off the bed. "The week, my heart. We will do this for a week, prepare for the autumn festival, and take as many breaks to make each other come as we need. You need this fat orc cock, don't you?"

"The week," I agree. "The week sounds good."

The sun's climbing outside the window before we take a long enough break to write a hastily scrawled sign declaring The Pixie's Perch closed to prepare for the festival.

The only thing I'm concerned about filling right now isn't a pastry at all.

CHAPTER FIFTEEN

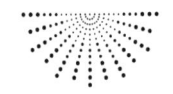

PIPER

The week's passed by in both a whirlwind of planning and preparations and cooking—and the best sex I've ever had in my life.

Not to mention the most caring, attentive male I've ever been in a relationship with.

Ga'Rek's quickly become my obsession, and the best part is, there is no question of whether or not it's mutual.

He hardly lets me lift a finger.

I hum a tune to myself as the charmed yeast pretzels come out of the oven. They're a last-minute addition to the fall festival feast line-up, a tiny appetizer to be passed around as party-goers filter into the makeshift tent we've erected over the town square.

It was a real pain to get it up, but the orange and black striped fabric our town's elven tailor managed to whip up looks incredible, lit from within with hundreds of charmed star-shaped lanterns.

Not only will the tent keep us out of the elements, should

temperamental Mother Nature decide to wreak havoc on us, but it also has turned the entire town square into a cozy, romantic venue.

I couldn't have done it without my coven sisters, without Ga'Rek, and without the rest of the town.

Every single being in Wild Oak Woods has come together to make this the best autumn festival yet, and while I am still incredibly stressed—I can breathe. I can relax; it's not just on my shoulders.

I am full of love for the creatures who have lifted me up, for Ga'Rek, for convincing me to ask for help, and for my fellow witches, who would have forced me to let them help whether or not Ga'Rek had been here.

It's been one of the best weeks of my life, and I know he's the one I have to thank for it.

I look to where he's normally working at his prep station, dominating the entire back counter, but he's not there.

I forgot.

Ga'Rek left early this morning, saying he had a last-minute errand to run.

A happy smile curves my lips at the mere thought of the soft way he kissed me goodbye.

"Piper," Wren calls from the front of the store.

Fenn the fox scampers into the back kitchen immediately, tilting his red-furred head and putting a white paw up the air. I chuckle, then toss him a bit of pretzel still hot from the oven.

He yips as he catches it mid-air, then rubs against my calves in thank you as he munches it.

"I'm back here," I yell. "Fenn already found me."

"Of course he did. And I'm sure he acted like he was starving."

"He would never," I tell her. I wipe my hands off on the tea towel, beaming at her and leaning my lower back against the countertop. "How are you?"

"Fantastic," she says. Wren bounces on the balls of her feet, a cloth pouch in her hands. "I brought you something. I made it."

Delight races through me. "You made me something?"

A gift from an enchantress witch is no small thing.

"It's the least I could do. I was inspired—" Her face falls as she goes quiet.

Bemused, I stare at her. "What? What's wrong?"

"I had a strange dream a few nights ago. That's all. Anyway, I dreamed that you were wearing these earrings, in that dream, and I decided you needed them."

My forehead furrows. Dreams are not always dreams, and I know Wren knows that as well as I do, so I just stare at her and wait.

She sighs, her chest heaving as she rolls her eyes towards the ceiling. "I know."

"You know what?"

"I know that you're going to tell me dreams can be visions," she says in an annoyed voice.

"I just want my jewelry," I tell her. "I can lecture you on dreams, too, or you can give me the gift and I promise to shut up."

She huffs a laugh at that. "Fair enough." The pouch is a deep sage velvet, and I take it from her gingerly.

"I love presents," I tell her, excited. "I know that's probably not the right thing to say right now, so thank you. But I love your art, and I am so thrilled you thought of me."

"That sounds like exactly the right thing to say to me. Keep talking." She preens, and I laugh.

"Go on," she says, snagging a soft pretzel from the tray, then tossing it between her hands and blowing. "Open it."

She doesn't have to tell me twice.

I pull at the corded drawstring, untying it and then delicately slipping a hand inside.

I gasp as I pull out a pair of lovely earrings, silver vines with tiny moonstone flowers.

"They're climbers. They sit vertically on your lobe and go up the sides. It's an elven design I decided to make witchy."

"They are gorgeous," I tell her.

They are, too, and she beams as I fasten them on my ears. "What charm did you use to enchant them?"

I can feel it, whatever the charm is, but what it's doing is unclear.

"Just whatever good thoughts I had while making them," she says, but her voice is unsure. "I've been working pretty hard, you know? I can't… remember. But I'm sure it's fine."

Her face clouds momentarily, and a feeling of foreboding passes through me.

The front bell rings, and Ga'Rek's heavy footfalls sound.

"You're back," I exclaim, my hands falling away from the earrings. "Good, it's nearly time to get ready and head to the festival. The duchess should be here soon."

Ga'Rek finally appears in the doorway, which he has to duck to get under.

I love how big my orc is, how safe I feel with him around, how protected.

He's carrying a brown paper parcel tied up with strings, and his cheeks are the deeper green color that means he's either excited or embarrassed.

"Oooh, looks like I'm not the only one who brought a gift," Wren says, waggling her eyebrows. "Okay, I'll let you two have some privacy. Make sure you wear the earrings tonight."

Her voice changes slightly, more commanding, but she wears the same smile as she slips out of the kitchen through the back door. "See you soon."

I frown at her retreating figure, something dancing in the back of my mind that I can't quite place.

"Here," he says, his voice gruff and not a little bit shy. "I'm sorry I haven't had the opportunity to get you something before now."

I laugh, then tsk at him. "Exactly, how dare you spend all week giving me the best sex of my life, making me feel loved, and helping me prepare for the festival? Uncalled for."

"I'm glad you feel loved," he whispers.

I hold my breath, waiting.

"I know it's early, I know I shouldn't say anything, but orcs... we aren't like humans. You are it for me, Piper, and I am falling in love with you."

I knock the parcel out of his hands and jump on him, showering his face in delighted kisses. "I love you too, Ga'Rek. I'm happier than I've ever been, and I like knowing where I stand with you. I don't want a human, or a fae, or a minotaur, or another orc. I want you. Only you."

I kiss him on the mouth, and it deepens, until he finally pushes me away with a laugh.

"We didn't work this hard to have you be late for your big event," he says.

"Fine." I roll my eyes. "Besides, you promised you were going to have your way with me at the event. Might as well save it for the right moment."

A guttural growl comes out of him, and I give him my best seductive smile.

Which, of course, makes him laugh.

"Here," he says, picking up the parcel from the floor and handing it to me.

"You do not have to buy me presents," I tell him.

He starts to say something, but I hold up a hand. "But I am very glad you did."

We both laugh at that, and I untie the string, then attack the paper wrapping.

Carefully, I lift the lid off the box, and my breath catches at what's inside.

"You got the dress?" I ask, my voice climbing an octave.

"I got the dress. That night, in fact. There was no way I wouldn't have gotten it for you." He grins.

I melt.

The midnight-soaked dress, spangled with silver thread stars, sits in the box, ready to be worn.

"I'm wearing it tonight," I announce.

"Good," Ga'Rek says, now grinning slyly. "Because I fully plan to fuck you in it. We don't have time now, though, so consider this a warning."

I glance at the clock on the wall and swear. "You're right. We need to hurry. We don't have time at all."

"Relax, sweetheart. You're going to be perfect as always."

"I am not always perfect," I say, grinning at his absurd statement.

He just stares at me seriously, cupping my cheek with his hand. "You are to me."

CHAPTER SIXTEEN

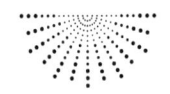

GA'REK

The autumn festival is unlike any event I've ever attended.

For one, there aren't any public tortures or executions, which is decidedly in Wild Oak Woods' favor.

There are, however, fire-eaters, who manage not to set the canvas tent on fire, thanks to a bundle of fire-proof enchantments we had Nerissa cook up around their stage. A dryad dances in suspended silks in another entertainment space, mesmerizing and attracting a large crowd. Two bards work the interior of the tent, one with a guitar and one with a fiddle, walking amongst the citizens and those who've driven in for the festival.

Caelan's inn is brimming with out-of-towners, and he's loving the challenge and the ability to bargain to his heart's content.

He's dancing with his lady love, who seems to laugh outrageously at every inane comment he makes as he twirls her.

Tables are set up in the back, festooned with pumpkins and

thick pillar candles, fall foliage and a shimmering autumnal spell we managed to convince Nerissa to make as well.

Piper's feast is laid out on the furthest table, under a set of spells of her own that she tinkered with all week to get just right, keeping hot dishes hot and everything at the perfect temperature.

Nearby, a stooped vendor's attracted a crowd of children, who crow in delight as he demonstrates magical toy after toy to them.

Piper's soaking everything in with wide eyes, resplendent in the dress I bought for her. Her hand holds my arm tightly, trembling with either excitement or trepidation or some mix of both.

"When is—"

An array of brass instruments interrupt and answer my question all at once, and Piper's fingernails dig into my wrist.

There's only one thing to do. I grab her face, lean down, and kiss her until her grip relaxes.

When I pull away, her lids are heavy, her lips swollen.

"What was that for?" she asks, blinking.

"To distract you from whatever was going on up there," I say, gently tapping her forehead.

She laughs, then shakes her head. "I suppose I approve, since it worked. Now I'm only thinking of one thing."

I lean down and inhale her. "I think I know what you're thinking of."

She laughs, and a woman in a cream-colored gown strolls into the tent, several burly guards around her.

"The duchess," Piper hisses, and a ripple goes through the crowd as everyone begins to acknowledge her presence.

"She's so young." Wren appears at Piper's side, frowning. "She can't be more than thirty."

"She looks scared," Piper says, her voice suddenly much stronger. "Come on, Wren, let's go see if we can make her feel at home."

They don't get the chance to.

Every occupant of the town square freezes, the duchess' eyes turning wide with dismay at the same time.

Three figures appear in the middle of the dance floor, and I realize all at once what it is that's drawn us all to Wild Oak Woods.

CHAPTER SEVENTEEN

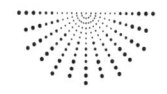

PIPER

I can't move.

From the mutinous, fearsome look on Ga'Rek's face, he can't either.

Wren and Caelan are likewise frozen, and it takes me a moment to think around my fear and notice that there are three huge forms in the middle of my carefully planned dance floor.

"You have summoned us, and we come to collect," a voice booms out.

The words must diminish their spell, because the crowd around them begins to scream and push each other in an effort to get away.

Nerissa's eyes glow where she stands at the edge of the dance floor, her gaze meeting mine.

The eerie feeling of déjà vu comes over me, and I try to raise my hand to cover my mouth.

One of the cloaked figures raises a hand, a hand tipped in talons, and the crowd falls silent again, freezing.

The vise of power clamps around my hand, staying it from reaching my face or anything else.

Nerissa's eyes glow brighter.

She's working a spell.

As one of the few truly powerful witches in our coven, she can work her magic without a word, without any potions or ingredients.

My attention flicks back to the cloaked, terrifying figures in the middle of the dance floor.

Nerissa makes a garbled sound, and her eyes have lost their glow.

"It has been a long, long time since mortals have summoned the likes of my brothers and I," the middle figure intones, and I shudder as he pulls back his hood.

Antlers jut from his head, arching back. His eyes are the deep green of primeval forests, mist-covered and ancient. He straightens, his gaze drifting to me, then through me, like he's pierced straight to the heart of my power.

"You request our power, our assistance, at the autumn solstice. You call us forth with charms," his eyes cut back to me, and horror pools in my stomach, "and the promise of new life."

The hulking figure on the right pulls his hood back, and it's the face of the most beautiful man I've ever seen—until his face shifts, turning into a desiccated skull. "With the promise of new life and protection, a pact is drawn. We give the power of the Elder Gods of the Elder Forest—"

"In return for the Witch Brides of Wild Oak Woods." The third figure pulls his hood down, and I can't look away. He's a swirling maelstrom, a mass of shadows and storms, violent and unpredictable as nature itself. Eyes like burning embers in a face that constantly shifts.

It's so surreal that it takes me a long moment to absorb what they've said.

"You have three weeks to prepare your chosen witch brides, or the Elder Forest will overrun Wild Oak Woods."

"I am promised to the Elder Forest." It's such a soft cry of a proclamation that at first I think I've imagined it.

But it's the duchess. The duchess, who looks so young and frightened that my heart might break for her.

The shadow man crooks a finger, and in the blink of an eye, the duchess, in her cream-colored gown, is at his side, her face terrified yet resolute as he wraps an arm around her.

They disappear without smoke or sound, like they were never here at all.

Two Elder Gods remain.

"Three weeks," the horned one intones.

Then they disappear, too.

The spell binding our movement melts away in horrible seconds, and my hands fly to my ears, because I know exactly the charm that called them here.

And Wren made them for me, with instructions from a dream.

CHAPTER EIGHTEEN

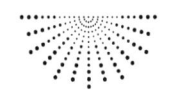

PIPER

"We're eating," I yell, suddenly furious.

It's mind-boggling that I'm managing to function at all.

"Are you out of your mind?" Nerissa yells.

I amplify my voice and my will, a spell I stumbled on as a toddler and drove my mother crazy with. "I went to all this trouble to cook, and we are going to enjoy ourselves." I level a finger at the duchess' guards, who don't look surprised, though they do seem slightly shell-shocked. "You. Come. Eat."

They don't move.

"Now," Ga'Rek roars.

The guards shuffle over to us, and Caelan and Kieran flank them as Ga'Rek points to a table.

The rest of my coven sisters have materialized around us, and even Violet, the new witch, so new we haven't even properly inducted her yet, walks towards us on shaky legs.

She looks how I feel.

"What the fuck?" Nerissa asks. "Did any of you do a summoning that went south?"

Ruby rubs her head. "There's no way. We would have felt it. And the duchess—she knew."

"You've never heard of this happening?" Damn it. I figured the bookstore owner was our best bet at knowing something.

"I've only lived here a handful of years," she says with a frown. "You've been here the longest."

"We moved here when I was a toddler."

"We all moved here... there has been no Wild Oak Woods coven in years," Willow whispers. "There have been no witches in Wild Oak Woods. Not for a long, long time."

"I suppose we can take a stab at why," Wren says wryly.

I glare at her. "Caelan is rubbing off on you."

"Stop bickering," Nerissa says. "The duchess knew. Let's interrogate her guards."

It seems like as good a plan as any. "I could enchant a roll with a truth charm?" I suggest.

"Good thinking," Nerissa agrees.

We make our way to where the guards are staring around.

"We don't know anything," one of them offers. "We're mercenaries. Hired to deliver a bride to a groom. No one said shit about any magic shit."

"A real master of language," Caelan says broadly. "Do you often provide armed escort to brides?"

"We take whatever jobs we can get. We're not weak and lazy like you townies."

Ga'Rek edges closer to the man. "Do I look weak or lazy?"

"Nah, I didn't mean anything by it," the guard—mercenary—amends hastily.

"I think I might be of assistance." A male dressed in all black shimmers into existence. Gold flecks sparkle along his skin, and his magic is as palpable as any I've ever felt.

Caelan laughs. He fucking laughs!

"Hash. Why am I not surprised to see you turn up?"

"Because you aren't as stupid as you look?" Hash says with a smile as sharp as a knife. "How is my Boner?"

"Don't fucking start that shit right now," Caelan tells him, more annoyed than I've ever seen.

"It's hard," Hash declares, taking a turkey leg off a plate and biting into it.

Caelan groans.

"It's hard to be in your position," Hash adds, his mouth full. "Summoning the Elder Gods of the forest like that. Having to hold the waypoint against the war for power that's coming."

He swallows, then tears another piece of meat off the bone. The Seelie fae has fangs, too.

Ga'Rek's edged over to me, positioning himself between me and the golden fae.

"We didn't summon any gods," Nerissa snarls.

"She did," Hash says, pointing a finger at Wren. His finger drifts over to me. "She helped."

My stomach sinks, and I have to remind myself to take a breath.

"A charm learned in a dream," Hash tuts. "You should know better, witchling."

"Can we leave now?" one of the mercenaries whines. Caelan smashes his elbow into his temple, and the man slumps over the table.

"Whoopsie daisies," Caelan says.

"Caelan, you can't just knock people out," Wren chides. "And I didn't... I didn't mean to? Doesn't that count?"

"No," Caelan and Kieran say at the same time.

"Witch brides are a powerful commodity," Hash continues like nothing's happened. "You should choose wisely."

"There's got to be a way out of this," Willow says quietly.

"There's not," Hash tells her. "You can either volunteer, or they will choose a bride for themselves in three weeks, and then also destroy Wild Oak Woods. Except for the old inn, of course. That's been there forever."

"The waypoint, you mean," Kieran mutters.

"Oh, you did figure it out." Hash claps his hands in delight. "Wonderful. Yes, yes, the waypoint, a focus point for power between the realms. Your mother did do well with you. Apple fell far from the tree and all that but here you are, growing into another apple tree."

I glance at Nerissa, confused, but she just stares at the golden fae.

"Why?" Ruby asks. "Why do they need witch brides?"

"Well, did you look at them? They're monsters. They're lonely, and witches are such fun. I'm fond of them myself."

He grins at us, then frowns when no one smiles back.

"That and the old Wild Oak Woods pact with the Elder Gods. It must be filled, you know. A power struggle is coming." His voice turns harsh, serious, and infinitely more terrifying. The lantern light, which I designed to be soft and cozy and inviting, throws harsh shadows across his face.

So much for that idea.

"Wild Oak Woods will be the battleground. The Elder Gods know this. This is how they offer their protection. You either take it and have a chance at keeping all your mortal friends alive, or you don't and everyone dies, and this hallowed place is still a battleground."

He shrugs, then beams again. "Either way, if you don't take the deal, you're dead."

"You're an asshole," Caelan tells him.

Ga'Rek wraps an arm around my waist, pulling me tight.

"That's why we get along so well, you and I, Caelan," Hash says brightly, then glances up at where Ga'Rek is baring his teeth at him. "Oh, don't worry, orc, they won't take a mated witch."

He glances around, as if cataloguing my whole coven. "The rest of you lovely, lovely witches, though, would make beautiful brides for the Elder Gods. Didn't the duchess look stunning? She was put out when I informed her family of her role in the matter, but I'm sure you can see she was well-suited for the role. A real power couple, that one." He nods.

"You did this," Wren accuses, rage making her words tremble. "You are the one who gave me the charm. You invaded my dreams."

"I didn't make you do anything. I just… nudged you towards it. Well, I'll be off," Hash says, clapping his hands together.

He disappears in a cloud of gold particles.

"Shit," I say.

"Shit," Wren agrees.

"Fuck," Ruby adds.

Violet and Nerissa just stare at the gold cloud where Hash was standing.

"We have some research to do. There has to be a way to break the summoning," I say.

"No." Ruby shakes her head. "The damned duchess already accepted their invitation."

"An invitation accepted is a spell performed," the rest of us say as one.

It's one of the first lessons you learn as a witch. An invitation accepted is as good as a binding contract in spellwork.

"Shit," I repeat.

"You could draw straws," Caelan suggests.

"Not right now, Caelan," Wren snaps.

"I could go," Willow says, and we all whip our heads towards her.

"Absolutely not," Kieran spits out. "I will not allow it."

"Why not?" Willow asks. "You don't think they would be satisfied with me as a bride? Is that it, Kieran? Not good enough?"

He looks shocked for a moment, like she's slapped him, but it turns into a sneer quick enough. "If you say so."

I gasp.

Tears well in Willow's eyes, and she turns, pushing past the few revelers left and running from the tent.

"That was rude," Caelan tells him. "Now she's just as like to offer herself up to spite you."

Kieran blinks, his lavender skin paling at the words, and then he's running after Willow's red curls, disappearing into the night.

"Okay, then," I say on an exhalation. "We have research to do."

"I can send word to the coven oversight committee—"

"No," Wren yells out, and we all startle. "No," she repeats. "Getting them involved is a bad idea. You have no idea how corrupt they are."

"I agree." Rosalina, the animal witch who cares for our familiars... and who has never once expressed any interest in anything we've done in town, stands at the edge of our fraught little circle. She tucks her hands into the pockets of her trousers. "The coven oversight committee is a bad idea. I can help." She raises her chin.

"Oh, now you can help?" I say. "How convenient for you."

"Some things are set in motion that we have no control over," Rosalina says, and her brown eyes are so sad that I almost find myself agreeing with her. "This is one of those things. I couldn't say anything."

"He cursed you into silence," Caelan chimes in. "That wily bastard. You struck a deal with him, didn't you?"

She nods, and there's no mistaking the sorrow etching lines into her forehead.

"I can help you navigate what's to come, but I might not be able to answer all your questions."

"That's something, at least," Nerissa says, somewhat recovered. "What do we do now?"

"Tonight? Tonight, I think, you enjoy each other's company. Enjoy the hard work that went into this beautiful event, and sleep well. Rest, and tomorrow morning, we will prepare for the storm that's brewing." She takes her time, meeting each of our eyes in turn. "Make no mistake about it, we'll each have a role to play."

Her gaze lingers on Violet for a fraction too long before she breaks into a small smile.

"It is good to have a coven in Wild Oak Woods again," she says.

I wrap my hand around Ga'Rek's.

I don't want to enjoy my event. How could I?

I want to go home and sit by the fire while my orc holds me. I lean into him, frightened.

"I have you," Ga'Rek whispers into my hair. "You are going to be okay. I will never let anything happen to you, kal'aki ne."

I close my eyes, relaxed, because I know truth when I hear it.

CHAPTER NINETEEN

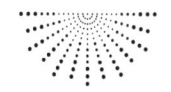

GA'REK

I am furious.

My Piper has spent so much time and energy on creating the most beautiful event I've ever seen, and now she's reduced tears and trembling frustration by a trio of forest gods no one can remember even hearing of before now.

"I'm right behind you," I tell her. "Let me just say good night to Caelan."

She nods, sniffling, and Wren shoots me a knowing look over her head. "Come on, Piper, I'll walk with you."

Her skirt rustles as she moves away, the once-festive and overfull tent now near empty, save for a few wide-eyed stragglers. Most of the vendors hustle as they attempt to close up their stalls.

"What magic do you have left?" I hiss at him.

Caelan's expression smooths out. "Do you want to strike a bargain, Ga'Rek?"

I roll my eyes towards the lanterns suspended from the

colorful waxed canvas stretched across the rooftops. Getting that right was a headache all on it's own, and now we can't even enjoy the night.

"I'll help," Nerissa, the black-haired witch, says. Her eyes glitter with anger, a muscle in her temple twitching. "What do you need?"

"I want to save the festival," I say, smashing one fist into my palm.

Her eyes go wide in alarm. "No need to hurt yourself. Goodness gracious."

"What can we do? I want everyone hear in the morning. A holiday. The festival. All the vendors. A Wild Oak Woods council meeting," I thunder. "A solution for Piper."

"Not just for Piper," Nerissa says, her lip curling. "A solution for all the unmated witches of the coven, I think you mean."

"Is there even a town council?" Caelan asks, looking thoughtful. "I don't recall Wren ever mentioning one."

"I…" Nerissa's voice trails off. "I don't think there is."

Something clicks. I blink. "And Piper has lived here the longest? Of anyone in town?"

A beat passes, where she's silent, and Caelan blows out a breath, his eyebrows shooting up.

"Of the witches, at least," Nerissa finally answers.

"We need to know the last time there was a coven here." I rake a hand through my hair. "There is a reason there wasn't one, and there is a reason there is now."

"History repeats itself," Caelan says slowly. "The inn?"

"The inn," I agree. "The waypoint. There must be—"

"A locus of power here," Ruby pipes up. "It's pulling individuals towards this location for a reason. The… three that showed up," she trips over the words, fear in her eyes, "they're a part of whatever is about to happen, whatever is happening."

"And you think it's happened before." Caelan glances sidelong at me.

"I can research. That's what I'm skilled at," Ruby says.

"We convene a meeting and enjoy the festival tomorrow," Nerissa agrees, raising an eyebrow. "We see if anyone is around who remembers the last coven, or if their grandparents do, or great-grandparents, and we hope one of them kept a journal."

Ruby nods in agreement.

"I can send a magical summons," Nerissa says, nodding. "And Ruby and I can work up a spell together to keep the food fresh."

"I'd like to help," Violet says quietly.

Hope begins to bud in my chest, and I inhale, nodding. "Good. We work together. We will need each other."

"I hope that's not the case. I was *so* beginning to like it here," Caelan says drily.

We all exchange irritated looks.

"Oh, lighten up, you lot." The fae rolls his eyes. "Of course we will work together. But you can count on me absolutely not taking anything seriously."

"Even Wren?" I ask.

He bares his fangs, and I laugh. Even Violet smiles.

"That's what I thought," I tell him, satisfied. "Pretend all you want, friend, I know there's a heart of gold in that wily body."

"I have had enough of this." He sniffs. "I won't be disparaged in front of my mate's coven."

Ruby covers her mouth, and emits a barking laugh that sounds something like a cough as Caelan stalks off, presumably to find his mate.

"We will weather this storm," Nerissa says somberly, her eyes glowing with a power that sends a cold shiver down my spine. "We will weather it, as the ones who came before us did. But make no mistake about it, a storm is building."

Violet goes pale, and Ruby throws an arm around her waist. "Don't worry. Nerissa loves to make dramatic proclamations."

Nerissa scowls, which makes the corners of Violet's lips twitch.

A chuckle escapes me despite the dire proclamation of the three forest gods.

"We'll make sure the festival is ready for tomorrow morning," Ruby assures me. "Go take care of Piper. We all know how hard she worked to make this happen. We won't let her efforts —or yours— go to waste."

My throat gets tight. "She's lucky to have you. We both are."

The witches only smile and shoo me off, beginning to discuss the details of how to make the festival go on tomorrow without a hitch.

I rush down the cobblestone streets to the Pixie's Perch and Piper's home, where the rest of my heart is waiting. A wicked cold wind blows from the south, shaking the trees that surround the small village until they scatter into the sky. Red and orange, they dance along the smooth stones.

The noises of Wild Oak Woods continue to surprise me. The sheer music of it; the wind in the leaves, the laughter and conversation of the creatures that live here, the conversations in the café. It's so different than the Underhill's mausoleum-like quiet.

The Dark Queen's Court was always taut with unspoken fear, hushed whispers and the cruel pronouncements made by the fae who held the Unseelie in her thrall.

My jaw clenches, and I quicken my pace, hunching slightly in an effort to avoid the icy wind blowing down the street.

I will not return to the Underhill.

This Wild Oak Woods is my home now, and I will protect it.

EPILOGUE

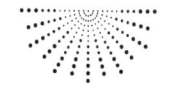

PIPER

I expect to sleep poorly, another night filled with nightmares and tangled in sheets, like when I was young.

When I wake up, though, Ga'Rek is there, curled around me.

One arm draped heavy around my waist, a tree-trunk thick thigh over my calves. His other arm's under my head, and the scent of his skin further relaxes me.

I wriggle closer to his warm body, and I know immediately the reason I slept so well is because he held me all night.

Ga'Rek probably scared all the nightmares away.

"Good morning, my sweet heart," he purrs in my ear. His lips brush against the skin there, and a thrill goes through me.

"Hi," I say sleepily, smiling.

When he presses against me, the hard length of him has me gasping.

"I have an idea of how we can wake up slowly," he says, kissing behind my ear and making me squirm.

I squint at the dwarven made clock and sigh heavily. "I have to help clean up the fall festival."

"No, you don't," he mutters.

"I do." I don't want to, but I push away from the captivating, delicious man and stand up. The floor's cold underneath my bare feet, and the wave of disappointment that rushes through me is even worse. I get dressed quickly, throwing on a warm pair of trousers and the thickest sweater I can find, because if my floors are this cold, that means the threat of winter's lurking in the wings and autumn's well and truly begun.

The coziest socks I have follow, and I finally locate my sturdiest pair of boots.

The floorboards creak as Ga'Rek gets up as well, putting on clothes of his own.

"You don't have to help," I say. "Stay in bed."

"As if I will choose to spend one moment away from your side."

I smile, closing my eyes as he holds me close, kissing the side of my neck. His tusks slide over my skin, and I sigh, wishing we could both crawl back in bed and hold each other the rest of the day. Funny, because I'm waking up much later than I usually do to open the bakery.

I suppose a gorgeous male and the promise of multiple orgasm could make anyone want to stay in bed all day.

I heave another sigh.

"Come on now, beautiful. It won't be so bad. You'll see. Or are you worried about the—"

I turn into him, cutting of his words by pulling his face to mine and planting a kiss on his mouth. I pull away, grinning at the way the corners of his eyes crinkle as he smiles.

"I am worried," I finally admit, and just telling him that, the simple utterance, takes some of the weight from my shoulders. "How could I not be?" I shake my head. "Those... whatever they were—"

"Elder gods," he supplies.

I snort, torn between amusement at both his knowledge and the cavalier way he says it —elder gods— and the fact that they are, in fact, elder gods.

Elder gods who want three witches from my coven.

Goddess have mercy.

"Do not worry, kal'aki ne. We will figure out a plan."

I sag into his embrace, hoping he's right. Hoping that we will figure out a plan.

The scent of roses fills the room, and I tug him to the windows that overlook the street. I grin at him.

"They're in full bloom."

Despite everything, the cold, the gloom in the grey sky overhead, and the terrible events of last night, the roses are in one last glorious flush before winter.

It feels like a promise.

꙳

I'M SO ABSORBED in staying warm and my own thoughts, that by the time we reach the square, I'm a knot of anxiety. Velvet trots next to me, her little tail flicking back and forth, looking adorable in a knobbly sweater I made for a her a few years ago during a particularly cold winter.

"Surprise!" a crowd shouts, all at once, and I look up, startled and somewhat terrified at what fresh hell might await.

Tears spring into my eyes, and I cover my mouth with both hands.

The tent is full of the citizens of Wild Oak Woods, and my witch sisters stand at the front, bundled up and beaming at me.

Willow twirls her hand in the air, signaling the musicians to begin playing again.

"How?" I breathe as they catch me up in excited hugs.

"I had the entertainers sign contracts in case of breach of

conduct," Caelan tells me from over Wren's blonde head, smug as a cat who caught the canary.

"A manifestation of a trio of gods is hardly a breach of conduct," I counter, slightly alarmed by the trickster fae.

"Ah, yes, but they signed it, and they did not fulfill their part."

"We're compensating them for any additional time," Wren adds, shooting Caelan a silencing look.

"Nerissa taught me how to preserve the food overnight," Violet adds, our shy new witch smiling hesitantly.

"And I've been working all night researching the last coven," Ruby adds. "And the Elder Forest, and the three gods who decided to party crash."

"Something they should leave to the experts," Caelan sniffs.

"I've been searching my plant lore to see if I can't concoct anything to protect the village," Willow adds.

Kieran looms near her, frowning, per usual.

"We're going to meet as a town once we've all enjoyed the festival and come up with a plan together," Nerissa says, her voice strong. Her eyes are strained, though, dark circles beneath them.

"Regardless of whether or not we're officially a coven, we are going to act as one." Ruby crosses her arms, a defiant cant to her head.

Ga'Rek laughs, one arm around my waist. "It looks just like you wanted, kal'aki ne."

I turn to him. "Did you know? Did you know they were doing this?"

"Aye, my love, I did."

"It was his idea," Nerissa chimes in.

I reach up to him, and he bends down, and when we kiss, in front of the entire town, who whoop and cry in response— it makes me think maybe, just maybe, everything will work out for the witches of Wild Oak Woods after all.

ALSO BY JANUARY BELL

FANTASY TITLES:

WILD OAK WOODS WORLD:

How To Tame A Trickster Fae
How To Woo A Warrior Orc

A CONQUEROR'S KINGDOM

Of Sword & Silver
Of Gods & Gold

FATED BY STARLIGHT

Following Fate: Prequel Novella
Claimed By The Lion: Book One
Stolen By The Scorpio: Book Two
Taurus Untamed: Book Three

SCIENCE FICTION TITLES:

ACCIDENTAL ALIEN BRIDES

Wed To The Alien Warlord
Wed To The Alien Prince
Wed To The Alien Brute

Wed To The Alien Gladiator
Wed To The Alien Beast
Wed To The Alien Assassin
Wed To The Alien Rogue

BOUND BY FIRE

Alien On Fire
Alien in Flames

ALIEN DATING GAMES

Alien Tides

ABOUT THE AUTHOR

January Bell writes steamy fantasy and sci-fi romance with a guaranteed happily ever after. Combining pure escapism, a little adventure, and a whole lotta love makes for romance that's a world apart. January spends her days writing, herding kids and ducks, and spends the nights staring at the stars.

For the latest updates, sign up for my newsletter by visiting www.januarybellromance.com, or follow me on Instagram and TikTok.

Printed in Great Britain
by Amazon